The Baby Experiment

Anne Dublin

The Baby Experiment

a novel

DUNDURN
TORONTO

Editor: Nicole Chaplin
Design: Courtney Horner
Printer: Webcom

Library and Archives Canada Cataloguing in Publication

Dublin, Anne
    The baby experiment / Anne Dublin.

Issued also in electronic formats.
ISBN 978-1-4597-0135-9

    I. Title.

PS8557.U233B33 2012   jC813'.6   C2011-906005-1

1 2 3 4 5   16 15 14 13 12

We acknowledge the support of the **Canada Council for the Arts** and the **Ontario Arts Council** for our publishing program. We also acknowledge the financial support of the **Government of Canada** through the **Canada Book Fund** and **Livres Canada Books**, and the **Government of Ontario** through the **Ontario Book Publishing Tax Credit** and the **Ontario Media Development Corporation**.

Care has been taken to trace the ownership of copyright material used in this book. The author and the publisher welcome any information enabling them to rectify any references or credits in subsequent editions.

J. Kirk Howard, President

Printed and bound in Canada.
www.dundurn.com

Dundurn
3 Church Street, Suite 500
Toronto, Ontario, Canada
M5E 1M2

Gazelle Book Services Limited
White Cross Mills
High Town, Lancaster, England
LA1 4XS

Dundurn
2250 Military Road
Tonawanda, NY
U.S.A. 14150

For my dear grandchildren

"Whoever destroys one life it is as though he had destroyed a whole world; and whoever saves one life it is as though he had saved a whole world."

— *Talmud* (*Mishnah*, Sanh, 4:5)

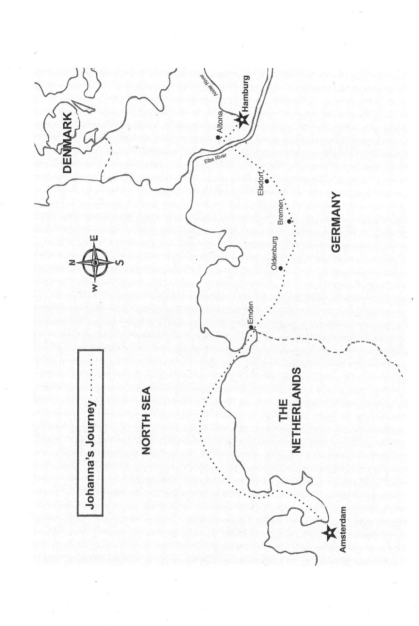

Chapter One

The Interview

Hamburg, Germany
1703

Johanna had been waiting on the hard wooden bench for over an hour. She shivered as cold drafts of air seeped in through the doors and windows. The hall was very grand with its tiled floor and faded tapestries, but it wasn't made for comfort.

She stood up, sat down, stood up again. She smoothed her dress and straightened her hat. She sat down again.

Johanna stared at the other girls sitting on benches that lined the hall. Some were chatting to each other; others sat stiffly, gazing at the walls or the floor.

Am I mad? Johanna thought. *Why did I come here? Perhaps if I do something, I'll be able to calm down.* She took a piece of lace out of her bag. She loved the way the bone shuttle drew the thread back and forth, making knots and creating a design. She had learned to do lacework like this from Grandmother Rachel. But her fingers trembled so much that, after a few minutes, she put her work away.

Last week, she had seen the announcement posted in front of the town hall:

> *Young women needed*
> *to work in orphanage —*
> *Under the sponsorship*
> *of the Duke of Brunswick.*
> *Apply in person*
> *at Hamburg Town Hall.*
> *Wednesday September 15, 9:00 a.m.*

Johanna felt guilty. She should have stayed to help Mama at the market. Every day they tried to sell the lacework she and Mama made, or notions like buttons and thread. On good days, they earned a few schillings; on bad days, they went to bed hungry.

Papa had been a stonecutter, specializing in headstones for the Jewish cemetery in Altona. Jews were forced to bury their dead there because they weren't allowed to have a cemetery in Hamburg. Papa often travelled between the towns.

Three months earlier, on his way home from Altona, Papa had been attacked by robbers. They had kicked him in the ribs and beat him on the head with heavy clubs, all the while calling him names like "dirty Jew." Some passersby had helped Papa get home. He lay in bed for several days until he succumbed to his wounds and died.

Papa hadn't been one of the wealthy merchants who had profited from trading tobacco, wine, cotton, or spices. Nevertheless, he was skilled with the chisel on stone. Now he himself lay buried beneath a stone in the Jewish cemetery where so much of his work stood.

Johanna helped Mama with the housework as well as at the market. But she hated cooking, cleaning, and washing! She was so tired of helping Mama! Today, Johanna had told Mama she was going to visit her friend, Marianne. Mama had grudgingly agreed.

Instead, Johanna had come here, to the town hall. She was sorry about lying to Mama, but if she got this job, she'd be able to buy a new dress or shoes or coat. More importantly, she would be able to give some money to Mama.

"Excuse me?"

Johanna was startled. She looked up into the blue eyes of a young woman sitting beside her. Her blonde hair hung in two neat braids on each side of her round face.

"Do you know anything about the new orphanage?" The girl twisted one of her braids through her fingers.

Johanna shook her head. "No. Nothing."

The girl smiled. "If I were as pretty as you," she said, "I would try to marry a rich man. Not look for work in an orphanage."

Johanna blushed. Mama always said she was pretty, with her auburn hair and hazel eyes, but Johanna didn't really believe her. After all, mothers always thought their daughters were beautiful. "You need a dowry to get married to a rich man," Johanna said, "and I don't have one."

"Nor do I," the girl replied.

"My name is Johanna. What is yours?"

"Cecile. Cecile Hansen."

"Are you from Hamburg?" Johanna asked.

"No. Altona." Cecile lowered her voice. "My brother, Antoine, is a merchant. He often travels between Altona and Hamburg on business. Last week he saw the sign posted outside. He told me about the job. So, I begged him to take me with him today."

"Perhaps we'll both be lucky."

"I hope so," Cecile answered.

A short man stood at the door at the end of the hall. "Next," he said and motioned Johanna to follow him. He wore a long, brown, full-bottomed wig. His jacket was light brown wool; his breeches, dark brown; and his buckled leather shoes were plain brown.

The windows' interior shutters had been opened wide and shafts of sunlight were playing with dust motes in the air. Johanna tried to walk quietly, but the sound of her shoes resounded loudly on the tiled floor.

The man sat down behind a large oak table. Beside him, a stout woman glanced up as Johanna approached. The woman wore a dark grey, woollen dress cut in severe lines. Her thin black hair was streaked with grey. Her small black eyes seemed to bore into Johanna's head, while her nose jutted out like a bird's beak.

Johanna couldn't find a comfortable place for her hands. She wanted to run away but her feet felt stuck to the floor. Her smile felt like the one painted on the Till Eulenspiegel puppet she had seen last summer at the Hamburg fair.

"What is your name?" barked the woman.

Johanna curtsied. "Johanna, if you please, ma'am."

"Last name?"

"Richter." Johanna had almost blurted out her real name, but stopped herself just in time. If she told them her name was Eisen, her real, Jewish name, she wouldn't get the job. People didn't give such work to Jews. To be sure, a few wealthy Jews lived in the city. But most Jews made their living in small trades — tailors, shoemakers, bookbinders. The Christians didn't trust Jews; they still believed all the old lies.

The man riffled through some papers on his desk and reached into his pockets, searching for something. Then he touched the spectacles resting on his nose, shook his head, and smiled. He dipped his quill into the inkpot, licked his lips, and wrote Johanna's name onto the paper. The scratching of pen on paper put Johanna's nerves more on edge.

"My name is Frau Taubman," said the woman. She pointed a fat finger at the man next to her. "This is Herr Vogel, the duke's secretary." The man nodded and pushed his spectacles farther up the bridge of his nose. "What is your age?"

"Fourteen."

"Do you have experience taking care of babies?" Frau Taubman asked.

Johanna swallowed hard. Her mouth felt dry as sand. "I had a younger brother and sister. I took care of them since they were babies. That is —"

"What?" Frau Taubman interrupted.

"They died last winter. Of the plague." Johanna's legs were shaking. She clenched her fists and willed herself to stand still.

"I see." Frau Taubman stared at Johanna. At her threadbare woollen dress, her frayed collar, and worn shoes. Johanna blushed under the woman's scrutiny. She was glad she'd washed her hands and face that morning. She hoped she didn't smell too badly.

"You seem to be a quiet one. You do not chatter on and on like some of the others."

"Thank you, ma'am," Johanna said.

"Now, girl, you need to understand something before you take this position."

"Ma'am?" Johanna's heart began to beat rapidly. *Does this mean she will offer me the job?*

"You will be responsible for the care of orphan babies."

"I know I —"

Frau Taubman pursed her lips and held up her hand. "We have a strict rule. An *unbreakable* rule. The caregivers will not be permitted to speak to the babies. And you may not hold a baby beyond what is absolutely necessary for its physical care."

"I don't understand," said Johanna. "Why not?"

"That is not your business," said Frau Taubman. "You must follow this rule." She narrowed her eyes. "Can you do so? And *will* you?"

Johanna nodded slowly. It was a strange rule, an unnatural rule, but she desperately wanted the job. "Yes, Frau Taubman. I can." She swallowed hard. "And I will."

"Very well, then. You shall be paid one thaler per month. Adequate room and board will be provided." Frau Taubman stared at Johanna as if she wanted to ask her another question but changed her mind. "Report to the duke's old summer house on the 27th of September. You will live there full-time, with one day off every three weeks." Frau Taubman paused. "Do you agree to these terms?"

"Yes, ma'am," Johanna said. Frau Taubman didn't seem like the sort of person anyone should disagree with.

"Make your mark on this paper," said Herr Vogel, sliding the paper towards Johanna. He handed her the quill, which she dipped into the ink. She signed her name — her false name — trying not to smudge the ink with her cuff.

"You know how to write?" he asked, raising his eyebrows. His spectacles slid down his nose.

"Yes, sir," Johanna answered. In a quieter voice, she added, "My grandfather taught me."

She was so grateful that Grandfather had taught her how to read and write. It was almost unheard of for a girl to have these skills. Grandfather always said that every person, man or woman, should know how to read. He said it was like a passport to another country. He once said something even more shocking — that everyone had the *right* to learn his letters. Grandmother had shushed him up at once for saying such an outrageous thing.

If Johanna had been a boy, she would have gone to *cheder* to learn. But girls were expected to stay home, and help with the housework and the children. If she were wealthy, she would have had a private governess. She wished she could study subjects like mathematics, geography, history, and other languages. But she was just a poor girl, with dreams beyond her station. Johanna bit her lower lip.

"An added bonus," Herr Vogel murmured. He handed Johanna a piece of paper. "Here are your instructions." He took his spectacles off and laid them on the table.

"You may go now," Frau Taubman said. She waved Johanna away, as if she were a pesky fly.

"Thank you, ma'am," Johanna said as she curtsied. Her legs were shaking so much she found it difficult to move.

"I wish you good fortune in your new job," said Herr Vogel.

"Thank you, sir," said Johanna, as she curtsied again.

"Perhaps you will need more than good fortune," he added.

His words puzzled Johanna, but she didn't dare ask him what he meant. She adjusted her cloak and tied her hat ribbons under her chin. She left the town hall and hurried outside.

"Fresh baked bread and rolls!"

"Get your chickens! Killed right before your eyes!"

"Fish! Fresh fish caught this morning!"

Farmers and craftsmen had set up wagons or carts on both sides of the street. As people walked from one stall to another, they tried to avoid stepping in dirty puddles or bumping into beggars. Those poor wretches sat on every street corner — their clothes in tatters, eyes hollow, and thin cheekbones jutting out from their faces. Papa had told her that people streamed into the city from the country. They were looking for work, but found only misery.

Children ran in and out between people's feet. Cats meowed, dogs barked, and large rats with gleaming eyes darted furtively along the narrow streets. Smells of old food and stale body odours, of rotten garbage and the contents of chamber pots thrown into open sewers blended together in a nauseating stench that permeated the air for miles.

But Johanna scarcely noticed the foul smells and loud din. She had a job! She lifted her long skirts out of the mud and walked as quickly as she could along the rutted road.

She had one problem. How was she going to tell Mama?

Chapter Two

Johanna Makes a Decision

Johanna stood outside the door to the room where she and Mama lived. She took a deep breath and let it out slowly. Then she pushed open the door.

Mama was kneading dough and didn't look up as she came in. "How is Marianne?"

Johanna turned her back to Mama and hung up her cloak.

"Why are you so quiet?"

"Mama, I have something to tell you," Johanna said as she untied the ribbons of her hat and hung it on a hook on the wall. "Mama," Johanna said as she walked closer to her. "I … I got a job."

Mama stopped kneading and looked sideways at Johanna. "What? What are you talking about?"

"I got a job." Johanna swallowed hard. "At the new orphanage."

"A job? At an orphanage?" Mama wiped the

sweat off her face with the back of her hand.

"The duke has given funds for a new orphanage and I saw a sign that they wanted girls to work there. I had an interview with Frau Taubman and I got the job," Johanna blurted out.

Mama put her hands on her hips. "You applied for a job and did not tell me?"

"Mama, I wanted to. I truly did," Johanna said. "But I didn't think you would understand."

"You are right. I do not." Mama began to knead the dough again. Blue veins like roads going nowhere criss-crossed on the back of her hands. "Where is this orphanage?"

Johanna sat down on the chair opposite Mama. She avoided looking at her and drew circles in the flour with her finger instead.

"In the new part of the city. In the duke's former summer house."

Mama sighed. "It is well and good that the high and mighty duke will sponsor an orphanage." Mama sighed again. "*But it is not for you.*" With every word, Mama pushed down on the dough.

"You should stay home like other girls your age. You should help me." She looked at Johanna sharply. "Besides, you know very well they would never hire a Jewish girl to take care of their babies." She frowned. "Unless ... Unless ..." She stopped kneading and lifted Johanna's chin with a floured hand. "Did you lie about being Jewish?"

"Not exactly," said Johanna, turning her head away and wiping her chin.

"Then *what* exactly? Johanna, look at me!"

"They asked me what my name was and —"

"And?"

Johanna could feel her face getting red. "I gave them a false name."

Mama shook her head. "So, you lied."

"But Mama," said Johanna. "If I hadn't, they wouldn't have given me the job!"

Mama sat down hard on a chair and crossed her arms. "You know how dangerous that is! If you get caught …"

"Mama, I won't. I'll be careful!"

"But why did you do it?"

"I want to earn some money. I see how hard it is for you since … since Papa died." She paused. "Besides, I want to be out in the world. I want to see new places, meet new people, learn new things." Johanna stood up and gazed out the window.

"The world?" Mama shook her head. "The world is not a kind place for Jews."

"I know, Mama," said Johanna.

"I wonder if you do." Mama took a handkerchief out of her apron pocket and blew her nose. "We are still being blamed for poisoning the wells, for spreading the plague, for …" She sighed and blew her nose again. "They can't decide why they hate us. All I want is peace and security."

Johanna walked over to Mama and wrapped her arms around her shoulders. "Please don't be angry."

Mama pulled away, stood up, and began kneading the dough again. "A respectable girl should stay home until she is married."

"But Mama!"

"Not one more word," said Mama, raising her hand. "You will contact this Frau …"

"Taubman."

"This Frau Taubman and tell her it was a mistake; that you have changed your mind."

"I can't," Johanna said.

"You must."

"I'm sorry, Mama, but I intend to take this job — with or without your permission."

Mama wagged her finger at Johanna. "You are stubborn," she said. "Since you were a little girl, you have always been stubborn."

"Not stubborn, Mama. Determined. There is a difference."

Shaking her head, Mama muttered, "Stubborn. Like a mule." She pounded the dough again and again, her knuckles pushing through to the wooden table top, her lips pressed tightly together. Finally, she shoved the dough into a pan, brushed melted butter on top, and threw a cloth over the pan. Johanna wondered if the poor dough would recover from its ordeal.

<hr/>

The following Saturday afternoon, Johanna and Mama were walking home from the house where some Jewish families gathered for prayers. *What would it be like to go to a real synagogue, built only for study and prayer?* Johanna wondered. *Would it be easier to talk to God in such a place? Would He listen to our prayers then?*

For many years, the Hamburg Senate had prohibited the Jews from building a synagogue. And now rumours were spreading that soon the Jews of Hamburg would no longer be allowed to practise their religion at all. Many of the wealthier Jews had already moved away — to Altona, Ottensen, and even as far as Amsterdam.

Lately, Johanna had been feeling as though a blanket of fear was suffocating her. She was afraid of being poor, and of being Jewish. For almost a hundred years, the leaders of the church had been demanding that the Senate expel the Jews. And for the past six years, the Jews had been forced to pay exorbitant fees for the privilege of staying in the city. *Will a day come when we will be thrown out of Hamburg?* Johanna wondered. *Where will we go? What will we do?* The thoughts buzzed in her head, like pesky flies she couldn't shoo away. Questions without answers.

"Johanna," Mama said. "I have been thinking. Are you still determined to take that job?"

"I am, Mama."

"It is not safe to live away from our community." She shook her head and blew her nose into her handkerchief. "Our only safety is to stay together; to follow our laws."

Johanna remembered when other children had

often taunted her younger brother, Isaac, on his way home from *cheder*; had thrown dirt or stones at him; had pushed the little boy into the filthy gutter.

"Mama, don't worry. I'll be careful. And I'll send you money every month to help out at home."

Mama put her arm around Johanna's shoulders. "I am trying to understand why you are so set on taking this job." She walked for several moments in silence. "You probably don't know, but when I was young, I wanted to see a bit of the world, too." She sighed. "It is hard for me, but I ... I will let you go."

"You will?"

"I see that you are set on this path." She shook her head. "Besides, no matter how hard I try, we are getting poorer and poorer. There is not enough money to buy food or clothes, or pay the rent. But Johanna —"

"Yes, Mama?"

"I will worry. Every minute you are away, I will worry."

"I'll write and visit as often as I can."

"I will still worry."

"But Mama, you always worry. About everything."

"That is true. But I cannot help my nature."

"And I can't help mine."

Most Jews lived in the section of Hamburg called "Neustadt," or New City, after they had been ordered to move from "Altstadt," the old city. Hamburg was a city intersected by two rivers — the Elbe and the Alster. It wasn't an easy city to walk, either, because of its many canals and bridges.

The duke's summer house was on the outskirts of the city, in a section Johanna had never been to before. Several times, she lost her way and had to ask for directions.

Dusk was falling as Johanna approached the brick mansion. Its wooden shutters were already closed against the coming night. Grey clouds scudded in a leaden sky. A cold wind was blowing the leaves off the beech and chestnut trees. Johanna shivered at the thought of the coming winter. And because of what lay ahead.

She remembered what Frau Taubman had said at the interview about not speaking to the babies. She'd pushed the thought away in her excitement about the job, but now the reality of what she had promised struck her like a blow. She sighed. *I must go forward*, she thought. *I've gone too far to back out now.*

A narrow, four-wheeled wagon stood in front of the cast-iron gate set in the fence surrounding the building. The driver leaned out of the wagon and tugged on the bell. Johanna imagined the sound echoing in all the rooms and corridors of the house.

"Hello there, girl." The driver peered at Johanna from under his battered cap. "What's going on here?" He eyed the building. "They told me to make a delivery. Couldn't wait 'till morning, they said. Said if I did this job, it'd be regular like."

"This is a new orphanage," Johanna said.

"An orphanage, you say?" The man rolled his eyes. "Still don't know what the hurry was." He scratched his head. White flakes of dandruff landed on his coat. "Why'd the duke go into the baby business?"

Johanna shrugged. "Perhaps he has a kind heart."

"Maybe." The man lowered his voice. "But they say his pocketbook comes before his heart." The man paused. "You work here?"

Johanna nodded.

"I'll be seeing you around then. Daniel is my name."

"My name is Johanna."

"Nice to meet you, fraulein," said Daniel, tipping his cap.

At that moment, Frau Taubman arrived at the gate. "There you are at last. You are late." She opened the gate and gestured Daniel inside. He glanced back at Johanna, shook the reins, and drove the wagon along the road to the back of the house.

"You too, girl," said Frau Taubman. "What took you so long?"

"I —"

"Come along now," Frau Taubman said. The clanging of the iron gate made Johanna's heart sink. *What have I gotten myself into?* she wondered. She followed Frau Taubman along the path and through a heavy wooden door.

They passed through a large foyer where an enormous painting of the duke hung. Bare spaces on the walls indicated places where other paintings had been removed. A richly carved pillar supported the ceiling, painted with religious scenes. Johanna had never been in such a grand room before.

A large-boned, rather plain girl of about sixteen approached them. "Monica, this is Johanna, one of the new girls," Frau Taubman said. Monica stared at Johanna but didn't answer. "Johanna will start work in the morning. Show her to her room."

"Yes, ma'am."

Johanna followed Monica up two flights of stairs. "Do you come from Hamburg?" Johanna asked.

"None of your business," Monica snapped. "I'm here to earn money. Not to make friends."

At the top of the stairs was a narrow hall with doors on either side. Monica opened the third door on the right. "This is your room."

The walls were covered with faded black and white striped wallpaper, which looked like the bars of a prison. A worn eiderdown quilt lay on the narrow bed. A small chest, table, and chair completed the furnishings.

"There's a chamber pot under the bed," Monica said. "The housemaid will empty it every morning. You must keep the room tidy."

"I will. I —"

"We start at 6:00 a.m., when we relieve the night girls. I'll tell you more about it tomorrow." Monica turned her back on Johanna and left the room.

Johanna began to take her meagre possessions out of her bag — clothes, handkerchiefs, toiletries. Just when she thought the bag was empty, her fingers grazed something else. At the bottom of the bag, she found Mama's lace kerchief, the one she wore when she lit the Sabbath candles on Friday evening. A note was attached to the kerchief, in Mama's childish script:

> My dear daughter Johanna,
> May you find light and luck in your new life.
> Be a good Jewish daughter. Keep the commandments.
> Stay warm and dry.
> Always keep a handkerchief in your pocket.
> With a heart full of love,
> Mama

For a moment, Johanna held the kerchief against her cheek. She could smell the faint scent of Mama's soap. She was suddenly overcome with homesickness. She had a sick feeling in the pit of her stomach, the one she got when she knew she'd made a terrible mistake. She desperately wanted to escape this strange place and rush back home.

Johanna gently placed the kerchief back into her bag. *I dare not light the Sabbath candles. If someone finds out I'm Jewish, I'll be fired.* She shivered. *Even worse, I might have to leave Hamburg forever because*

I pretended to be a Christian. Then a thought struck her, like a blow to her stomach. *I am doing exactly what Grandfather Samuel did. I am hiding my Jewish identity in order to survive.*

She gazed out the window as she ate the bread and cheese she had brought with her. The spires and domes of the nearby churches — St. Michaelis, St. Jacobi, St. Petri, St. Nicolai, and more — towered above houses and shops stretching away from the harbour on the banks of the Elbe River.

Johanna tried to shake off her feeling of uneasiness. It was strange being alone in this room, in a bed she didn't have to share with Mama, in a room all her own. For a long time, she had trouble falling asleep.

— Chapter Three —

At the Orphanage

Johanna woke to the sound of shouting outside her room.

"What do you mean you did not have time?" Frau Taubman's voice seemed to bounce off the walls. "When I tell you to do something, I mean do it, and do it *now*."

"Yes, Frau Taubman," a girl said in a quivering voice.

"Why are you standing there, gawking at me?" A loud slap jolted Johanna fully awake. "Now go!"

"Yes, ma'am." The girl's sobs faded away down the hall.

Trying to shake off a feeling of foreboding, Johanna stood up and groped for the chamber pot. In the near-dark, she walked to the washstand and poured cold water from the pitcher into the basin. She washed her hands and face, and dried them with the rough linen cloth hanging from a hook on the wall. Johanna shivered. The room still held last night's chill. She got dressed as quickly as she could. She ran a comb through her thick hair, attached it in the back with a leather clasp, and walked down to the foyer in search of breakfast. Following the clatter of pots and pans and the smell of porridge cooking, Johanna found her way to the spacious kitchen.

A stout woman was standing in front of the stove. She was stirring something in a large copper pot. She looked up and noticed Johanna standing at the door.

"Come in," said the woman, gesturing with a wooden spoon. "You must be the new girl."

"Yes, ma'am. My name is Johanna Richter."

"I'm Frau Hartmann. Sit down over there. I'll give you your breakfast in two shakes of a lamb's tail." Frau Hartmann pointed to a rough wooden table with a bench on each side where two girls were already sitting. Monica glanced up at Johanna.

"Johanna!" The other girl said. Her eyes lit up when she recognized Johanna.

"You're —"

"Cecile."

The girl nodded. "From the town hall."

Johanna sat down opposite Cecile. "When did you get here?"

"The day before yesterday. And you?"

"Last night."

Frau Hartmann placed a steaming bowl of oatmeal in front of Johanna. "Here. Eat. It looks like you need some fattening up."

Johanna remembered the old story of the witch who lured children into her cottage. She fed them cakes and cookies — and maybe oatmeal? — to fatten them up so she could eat them. But Frau Hartmann didn't look like a witch. Johanna shook off her overactive imagination. She blew on the oatmeal, poured some milk on it, and started eating while Cecile cut slices of rye bread.

"So, what is it like here?" Johanna asked Cecile as she reached for a piece of bread. She felt famished — yesterday she had been too nervous to eat much more than the bit of bread and cheese she'd brought with her.

Cecile glanced towards Monica. "It's fine," she said.

"How many babies are there?"

"Ten, so far. Six girls and four boys."

"Why are there more girls than boys?" Johanna asked.

"I don't know."

"I do," Monica said, banging her spoon on the table. "Because girls aren't worth as much as boys."

"What are you talking about?" said Johanna. "Of course we're worth as much!"

"And more," added Cecile.

"That's what *you* think!" said Monica. "Some people think that girls are only good to get married, do housework, and have babies. Boys can work in the fields, or learn a trade."

"I wish *I* could learn a trade," said Cecile.

"People shouldn't give their babies away, just because they're girls," Johanna said.

"Maybe not, but they do." Monica shrugged. "Anyway, it doesn't matter. These babies are foundlings. Their parents are dead. Nobody wants them."

"I don't think —" Johanna said.

Just then, Frau Taubman strode into the room. She glanced at the half-eaten breakfasts on the table and grabbed a piece of bread. "There you all are. Aren't you finished yet?" she barked.

Johanna tried to stuff the rest of the bread in her mouth. *Mama always said it was a sin to waste food. This is my first day here, and I'm already breaking a commandment.*

"Yes, Frau Taubman," the girls replied quickly, as they stood up.

"Come along then," Frau Taubman said, gesturing impatiently for the girls to follow her.

"Haste makes waste," muttered Frau Hartmann as she gathered up the dirty dishes.

The girls followed Frau Taubman along a wide corridor. The keys hanging from her belt jangled with each step she took. At the end of the corridor, they entered what once must have been the grand ballroom. Now it served as the nursery.

Johanna counted six cribs along one wall, six along the other. A wooden partition separated each crib from the one next to it. Babies were crying, some more loudly than others. Three girls were sitting in various parts of the room. They stood up and walked to the door as the group entered.

Frau Taubman dismissed them with a wave of her hand. "Monica," she said, "tell the new girls what to do. I have other duties to attend to." She paused. "And remember. No talking to the babies or to each other, no singing or humming. Absolutely not one word." Frau Taubman left the room in a swish of black silk.

How could I have forgotten? Johanna thought. *How can I not talk or sing or hum to the babies? It's not right. It's not fair. It's not even human.*

Monica pointed to some shelves. "The wet nurses leave the milk in these bottles for the babies every morning. Diapers, blankets, and clothes are in the linen closet. Each baby has a sign on its bed, showing its name and birth date, if we know it, and its measurements, like weight and height. Doctor Keller measures them every Monday."

"Who's Doctor Keller?" Johanna asked. "Does he take care of the babies?'

"Yes," said Monica. "But it's really Professor Gottfried Leibniz who's in charge of this experiment."

"Experiment?" Johanna's heart skipped a beat.

"Sure. What did you think this was?"

"I thought …" Johanna said. "I thought this was a regular orphanage."

"I did, too," Cecile said, twisting one of her braids.

"Don't think too much around here," Monica said. "You'll be better off."

"But —"Cecile said.

"But nothing." Monica continued with her instructions. "There's lots of other things you need to know. So be quiet and listen. We're each assigned our sections. That's Johanna's," she said, pointing to the far end of the room, "and that's Cecile's," pointing to the middle section. "Mine's here near the door. You can sit or stand or walk around, whatever you want. When a baby cries, you take care of it. Change its diaper, feed it, things like that. Just remember —"

"No talking," both girls said at the same time. They started to giggle until Monica gave them a hard look.

"Stop it. It's not a joke," Monica said. "Now let's get to work."

They walked to their sections. Johanna read the names of her babies: Rebecca, Angela, Gertrude, and Joseph. They were all about the same age, between one and three months old.

During the next few hours, Johanna learned more about her charges. Rebecca was the oldest and the most restless. She liked to lie on her stomach, raise her head, and look around her with big, blue eyes. Wisps of thin blond hair covered her almost-bald head and she held onto Johanna with a fierce grip. Joseph and Gertrude cried almost constantly. Angela lay quietly in her crib, and didn't seem interested in anything.

Johanna was determined to take good care of her babies, but it was harder than she had expected. No sooner was one baby quiet than another one would begin to fuss and cry. She felt like the juggler she had seen at the fair last year. She wished she could work on her lace, but at first she was too busy and then she was too tired.

A servant brought them lunch — bread, cheese, and milk. Later, another maid came into the nursery and took out the baskets of dirty diapers and clothes for washing. Johanna felt as if the day would never end. Finally, as it grew dark, the night girls arrived and the day girls were allowed to leave the nursery. They walked to the kitchen for the evening meal.

They washed their hands at the washbasin and sat down at the table. Johanna was amazed by the luxury she saw around her. Water was piped into the kitchen, and a huge earthenware stove called a *kachelofen* was used instead of the fireplace and hearth Johanna had at home.

"What do you think?" Cecile asked, looking around to make sure Monica was out of the room.

"It was a long day," Johanna said.

"For me, too," Cecile said. "It doesn't seem natural, to be so quiet around babies."

"I know. I wanted to talk to the babies. I had to stop myself every minute."

"I felt the same. You know, I'm used to talking a lot. Mother calls me a regular chatterbox."

"Not me. I like to read or work on my lace," Johanna said.

"Then this place must be perfect for you."

"I guess. But it's hard for me to be so quiet with babies, too."

Just then, Monica walked into the room. "What's going on?" she asked.

"Nothing." Cecile said.

"Well, in that case," Monica said. She sat down on the bench opposite the girls, a sullen look on her face.

"Here's your supper," Frau Hartmann said.

"What's this?" Johanna asked, poking at a pale object in her stew.

Frau Hartmann answered, "Why, they're potatoes, my dear. Have you never eaten 'em before?"

Johanna shook her head. "At home, Mama made stew with cabbage and onions, and sometimes turnips or carrots."

"Try them. They're delicious," Frau Hartmann said. "My cousin grows them on his farm in Alsace. He says they're like manna from heaven."

"This stew isn't manna, and this orphanage isn't heaven," said Monica. "Anyway, potatoes give me gas."

"Watch your tongue, young lady," said Frau Hartmann. "In my kitchen, I expect good manners."

"Sorry." Monica glared at Frau Hartmann, lowered her eyes, and picked at her food with her spoon.

"Try it," Cecile urged. "We grow them in Denmark, too. They're good."

Johanna had heard people talk about potatoes. They said you could get sick from eating them; that you might even catch leprosy. She looked over at Cecile and decided. "All right. I will." She picked up a chunk of potato with her spoon, blew on it, and chewed it slowly. "It's delicious!"

"It *is* delicious," said Cecile, between bites. "Frau Hartmann, is this pork? It's my favourite!"

"Why yes, my dear. I was lucky this morning. Those were the last pork hocks the butcher had."

Johanna choked on the food in her mouth. She started to cough.

"What's wrong with you?" asked Cecile. "You look green."

"It's nothing," said Johanna, putting down her spoon. "It went down the wrong way." Vomit rose in her throat. *How could I have been so stupid?* she thought. *How could I have forgotten that the food here wouldn't be kosher? I can't eat pork. It would break all the rules I grew up with. But if I don't eat it, they'll know I'm Jewish.* Only one day had passed, but she wanted to get up and run away and never see this place ever again.

Monica was looking at her strangely. "You act like you've never eaten pork before."

"Of course I have," said Johanna. She could feel her face getting red. "It just went down the wrong way."

"Well, if that's all it is," said Monica. She leaned forward and waved her spoon in Johanna's face. Johanna could smell the sour sweat from her unwashed body. "You'd better not be one of those Christ-killing Jews."

"Leave her alone," said Frau Hartmann. "Eat your supper."

Johanna couldn't speak. She could only shake her head. She felt ashamed — not because she was Jewish, but because she was pretending not to be. She sighed. She suspected that pretending not to be Jewish would be more exhausting than she had imagined.

"My brother says you can't trust Jews," said Cecile. "That they're always trying to cheat him."

"I hate Jews!" said Monica. "They're dirty and always smell horrible."

"I heard," Cecile whispered, "that they have horns and a devil's tail."

"That's so backward!" Monica sniffed. "People don't believe that anymore. Shows you're from the country."

"I'm not! I'm from Altona!"

"Country enough."

"It's not!" said Cecile.

"That's enough chatterin' like a bunch of foolish birds!" said Frau Hartmann. "Be quiet and eat this good food I cooked."

Johanna couldn't listen to the horrible things they were saying about her people any longer. "I'm not hungry," she said as she stood up. "I'm going to my room."

"What's the matter with her?" Monica said as Johanna hurried away.

Chapter Four

The Experiment

As the weeks passed, the babies started to die. George, one of Cecile's babies, was the first. For days, he lay in his crib, without crying, without even whimpering. Most of the time, his eyes were closed. But even when they were open, he stared straight ahead, as if he wasn't seeing anything. He sucked listlessly on his bottle, and eventually he refused to eat at all. After a few days, he was dead. Cecile wrapped him in a linen sheet and placed his tiny body into a plain wooden coffin. Since then, Cecile's eyes were always red from crying. She kept saying she wanted to go home.

Stephanie, one of Monica's babies, died a few weeks later. Monica walked around all day long, a scowl on her face and angry words on her lips.

Now Angela was very ill. Johanna had trouble concentrating. She was constantly spilling milk, breaking things, tripping over her own skirts.

Frau Taubman became more and more demanding. She blamed the girls for the babies' deaths and had no patience for even the smallest matters.

With each sick baby, Doctor Keller tried every remedy he knew. He prescribed medicines and tonics. He bled them to rid them of bad humours. He placed leeches on their thin tummies and legs. He put hot glass bottles on their backs. They screamed in pain, but nothing helped.

One day, Johanna was returning from the bathroom when she heard Doctor Keller and the scientist, Professor Leibniz, arguing in the hallway outside the nursery. She hid in a doorway as she listened.

In spite of his fashionable clothes, Professor Leibniz didn't make a striking impression. He was a thin, middle-aged man whose long nose jutted out from a face as pale as a turnip. His limbs were crooked and ungainly; he carried his head far forward of his hunched shoulders.

It was said of him that he often stayed in his chair for days at a time while he was working on his various theories and projects. It was whispered that he was brilliant, ambitious beyond reckoning, and an inveterate liar.

"I must know what is wrong with the babies," Leibniz was saying.

"I cannot understand what is making them so sick," said Doctor Keller. "They do not seem to have an illness that I can diagnose. They are simply not growing as normal babies should." He paused. "I wonder why they do not thrive."

"Thrive?" Leibniz said, straightening his black wig. "You did not obtain this position to ask questions. Only to follow orders."

"Listen to me for a moment," said Doctor Keller. "The babies have little appetite. They are not gaining weight. They lie listlessly in their beds and show little curiosity about the world around them. I cannot but think that the babies have given up the will to live."

"You must find out what is wrong with them," said Leibniz. "You must bring them back to health. They are vital for my experiment." Leibniz paused and rubbed his hands together.

"Experiment?" Doctor Keller said. "The babies are *dying*. Whatever it is, you must stop this experiment at once."

"That is impossible," said Leibniz, sniffing. "The price of knowledge is unfortunately sometimes very high."

"But Professor ... *this* price is far too high." Doctor Keller took a large handkerchief out of his pocket and wiped his sweating face. "What kind of experiment are you conducting, Professor Leibniz, that makes it worth the lives of these poor babies?"

Johanna's heart was pounding as she eavesdropped. She was terrified that she might be discovered.

"I have a theory that all languages come from one and the same language — what I call a 'proto-language.'" Leibniz said.

"A proto-language?"

"Yes. I believe that all languages have one common ancestor — not Hebrew or Swedish, as some people propose. Something else." He paused. "I am certain I will discover it through this experiment."

"I see," said Doctor Keller. "But ... what about the babies?"

Now Johanna was sure. This was no ordinary orphanage, but the setting for an experiment — one that was proving deadly. *No one has the right to experiment on human beings*, Johanna thought. *Does Leibniz think that science is more important than people?* She felt she would burst with the effort of keeping silent.

"It is your responsibility to see that my subjects receive the very best of care — food, shelter, clothing." Leibniz raised his voice. "Do you perhaps think that the caregivers do not tend to them properly?" Johanna pressed herself against the wall.

"Not at all," said Doctor Keller. "The caregivers are competent. The babies must also be talked to and held and loved. It is only common sense. You are denying the babies their emotional needs." He paused. "Your theory," Doctor Keller said scornfully, "your theory prevents me from treating them properly."

Leibniz wagged a finger at Doctor Keller. "And you prevent *me* from conducting this important experiment. Do not forget: the duke has agreed. He is my sponsor." He sniffed unpleasantly. "Doctor, if you cannot determine what is wrong with these foundlings, then we will find someone who can."

"As you wish," said Doctor Keller, bowing. "Do so. Seek another physician. I am done with this wretched business." Johanna heard his footsteps and peeked around the corner.

"Wait, doctor!" called Leibniz, lurching after Keller. "Please come back! I did not mean that you *should* stop caring for these babies."

"Then what did you mean?" asked Doctor Keller. His usually red face was becoming redder; his waistcoat buttons seemed about to pop.

"Only that we must both work together for … the welfare of these poor unfortunate babies."

"It is obvious that our ideas about their welfare differ in the extreme," said Doctor Keller. He was almost a head taller than Leibniz and stared down at the ugly scientist with disdain.

"That may well be true. But we can still work together, can we not?"

"Perhaps."

"Of course we can! After all, are we not both learned men of science?"

"We are." Doctor Keller's voice shook.

"Good. Then we are agreed." He cleared his throat. "By the way, have you heard about the new Academy of Sciences in Berlin? I am its first president, you know. And have I told you about my plan to drain the canals in Venice…? No? Have you been to the Gänsemarkt, the new opera house? Tomorrow, I plan to see the debut of that young composer — Handel, I believe is his name."

Their voices faded as they walked down the hall

away from the nursery. The strong scent of Leibniz's cologne lingered in the air. Johanna waited until they had gone and hurried back to the nursery.

The situation at the orphanage continued to worsen. The babies had little appetite, so they lost weight and weakened. Some of the babies were listless and apathetic; others were angry and irritable. No matter how they acted, the result was the same. The undertaker's wagon became a familiar sight at the orphanage.

One of the night girls quit and had been replaced. An air of despair and depression filled the grand rooms and corridors of the mansion. *Once this must have been a place of joy and laughter*, Johanna thought. *Now it is a place of death.*

It was not the kind of death that takes a person at the end of a long, well-lived life. These small, helpless babies died before they had a chance to live. *What would they have become?* Johanna wondered. *Whom would they have married? What good work would they have accomplished?* She felt sick when she thought of these needless deaths. She wished she could do something, but felt paralyzed with fear and doubt.

Autumn dragged slowly into winter. Johanna knew she was a liar for hiding her identity. But now she had also become a thief.

Yesterday, when she had finally visited Mama, they talked for a long time. Mama looked older somehow, with deeper lines on her face and more grey hair sprinkled among the black. They sat in the dingy room and drank tea while Johanna told Mama about the babies.

"It is a terrible thing to see babies die," Mama said. She closed her eyes and leaned her chin on her hand. Johanna knew she was thinking about her own children that she'd lost. Suddenly, Mama opened her eyes and grabbed Johanna's arm. "Are you lighting the Sabbath candles? Are you keeping the commandments?" She sighed and dropped her hand onto her lap. "I worry what will become of you in that place."

"I try to, Mama. I try, but I can't always do it."

Mama pursed her lips. "It is Hanukkah this week. Have you been lighting the candles?"

Johanna shook her head.

Mamma stood up, rummaged on a shelf, and grabbed something. "Here. Take these," she said as she dropped nine small candles onto the table. "Light these, at least. Tomorrow is the last night."

"I will, Mama," said Johanna. "I will."

The sun was setting as Johanna crept up to her room the next night. She had stolen an old pan from Frau Hartmann's kitchen. She took the pan and set it on the table. She placed eight candles in a row on the pan, struck a match and lit the ninth candle, then used that candle to light the other eight. She said the blessing and gazed at the candles, their light shimmering in the dark room.

Johanna loved the story of Hanukkah; how it represented rebellion against great odds; how the Jewish people had always yearned for freedom against oppression. The story told of a miracle that had taken place in Jerusalem a long time ago. *I can't expect miracles here*, Johanna thought. *The only miracle will be one that I make for myself.*

Johanna heard steps outside her room and voices whispering. She imagined they were talking about her; suspecting her of being Jewish; declaring that she had no right to work at the orphanage, to live in Hamburg, to be free. The voices were coming closer. Johanna sighed, took a deep breath, blew out the candles, and hid the stolen pan under her bed.

———◆◆◆———

The months passed. After baby Angela died, Doctor Keller ordered all the windows shut to avoid drafts. Johanna felt smothered in the closed atmosphere of the nursery. She needed to get away from the noise of crying babies. She needed to breathe fresh air.

One day in early spring, Johanna walked out to the garden at the back of the house, where the land sloped gently downwards. Birches, oaks, and chestnut trees dotted the hill. Delicate green buds were bursting on the trees. Birds of all kinds — sparrows, finches, and larks — sang in the trees as they looked for morsels of food and choice materials to build their nests.

Those birds act like Mama on market day, choosing only the best quality the merchants have to sell, thought Johanna. It had been months since she'd felt her mother's arms around her. The work at the orphanage was exhausting. She rarely had the energy to go home during her days off anymore. But she wrote to Mama regularly, enclosing money each time.

Johanna couldn't forget what Doctor Keller had said to Leibniz months earlier. Lately, she'd tried an experiment of her own. She wondered whether she could reverse the effects of Leibniz's experiment; whether she could help a baby thrive. When no one was looking, she held baby Rebecca longer than she was supposed to. She cuddled her, and gave her hugs and kisses. She sang a lullaby she remembered Mama singing to her:

> *Sleep, little baby, safely sleep.*
> *The birds are singing in the woods.*
> *They sing and hop in the grass so green.*
> *They'll bring the baby something good.*

Like a wilted flower opening to the gentle rain, Rebecca began to respond. She made cooing and gurgling noises. She stared at Johanna as she listened to her whispered words. Her big eyes were like a bird's, alert and curious. Rebecca was growing prettier, too. Her hair was becoming softer and her skin was losing its pallor. Every day, Johanna looked forward to seeing Rebecca, to holding her in her arms and whispering to her.

Johanna knew she was breaking the rules but she no longer cared. No amount of money was worth seeing the babies die. Nothing was.

Johanna sighed, sat on a bench in the garden, and opened her Bible. She was reading the story of Moses — one of her favourites. Because of a prophecy, the pharaoh in Egypt had given the order that all Hebrew baby boys must be killed. Miriam hid behind some reeds and watched as her baby brother floated in his basket on the Nile River. An Egyptian princess found him and raised him as her son.

Johanna's heart started pounding. Although she had read this story many times before, today it was as if the words on the page spoke directly to her. *I could be like Miriam was to Moses. I could take Rebecca away from this horrible place.* She closed her eyes and tried to imagine what it would be like. *What if I ran away with her? I would have to find somewhere safe for us. And then I could adopt her — just like the Egyptian princess adopted Moses!*

Johanna shivered in spite of the warmth in the garden. *I am not brave. Can I save Rebecca and still help Mama?* She plucked a blade of grass and shredded it with her fingernail.

It was an impossible choice, but Johanna knew it was one she must make. *I will do it. No matter how dangerous the journey might be.* Her heart skipped a beat. *Where can I go? It must be far away. Mama must not get into trouble because of me.*

Grandfather Samuel had told her of a city where Jews could become citizens. He had called it the "Dutch Jerusalem." He had told her that Jews could worship in freedom there; that they had even been allowed to build a synagogue. Johanna clenched her fists. She would go to that city. She would go to Amsterdam.

Johanna hurried back inside the house, her head buzzing with all the things she must do to prepare for the journey. *Grandfather, I remember the stories you told me about how you ran away and made a new life in a new land. You had courage. Will I have courage, too?*

Chapter Five

Johanna's Plan

Daniel, the wagon driver, had come to the orphanage to make his regular deliveries of fruits and vegetables. "You want to do *what*?" he asked.

"Shhhh!" whispered Johanna. "I want to leave this place." She knew she could trust Daniel, because he'd delivered money and letters to Mama.

"Why do you want to do such a foolish thing?" said Daniel. "You've got a good job here. A place to sleep. Regular meals. Steady pay."

Johanna shook her head. "Daniel, the babies are dying. Six babies have died already."

Daniel took off his cap and scratched his matted hair. "I know. Ain't I the one who delivers the coffins here?"

"Three more babies are very weak. I think they're going to die soon." She swallowed hard and tugged on the sleeve of his jacket. "I want to run away and —"

"Run away? Why not just quit the job and leave?"

Johanna lowered her voice. "I want to take one of the babies with me."

"You must be crazy!" Daniel shouted.

"Please be quiet!"

Daniel peered at Johanna. "Where to?"

Johanna looked over her shoulder. "First to Altona. It's safer there. Then I'll look for a ship to take me to Amsterdam." She paused. "Will you help me?"

"Can't. Won't. I'd get in trouble for sure. They'd lock me up for aiding and abetting a kidnapper!" Daniel blew his nose onto the ground and wiped the snot with his sleeve.

Johanna handed Daniel her handkerchief. He took it as if he didn't know what to do with it. He crumpled it up and shoved it into his pocket.

"Please, Daniel."

Daniel shook his head. "I won't do it. I feel sorry for the babies, but I ain't gonna take that kind of risk." He grasped the reins and began to move away.

"Wait!" Johanna cried. "I'll pay you!"

Daniel stopped and stared at Johanna.

"I'll pay you for taking us — me and the baby."

Daniel scratched his head. "Well, if you're talking business, that's something else. How much?"

"Twelve schillings?"

"Twenty-four."

Johanna swallowed hard. "Eighteen. That's my final offer."

"Well, I guess that'd be enough."

"You'll take us, then?"

Daniel nodded. "Only as far as Altona. My horse is old and I got my regular customers."

Johanna let out her breath. She hadn't even realized she'd been holding it. "Thank you."

Daniel stretched out a dirty hand towards Johanna. "Let's see your money."

Johanna shook her head. "I'll pay you nine schillings when you pick me up and nine when we reach Altona. Agreed?"

Daniel scratched his armpit. "You drive a hard bargain. All right then." He shook his head and murmured, "I must be as crazy as she is."

"When will you be back here again?" Johanna said.

"Let's see." Daniel counted on his fingers. "Today's Thursday. It'll be Monday next."

"Johanna! Where are you?" Cecile called from the doorway.

Johanna waved at her friend. "Coming!" She turned back to Daniel. "When you finish your deliveries on Monday, wait for me outside the gate behind the high hedge. I'll meet you after breakfast."

"What if someone asks what I'm doing there?"

"Johanna!" Cecile was walking towards them. "I've been looking all over for you."

Johanna moved closer to Daniel. She could smell his sour, unwashed body and the dirty wool of his clothing. "Say you were taking a nap, or reading a book, or feeding your horse. Whatever you want."

"Right. But if you ain't here by seven o'clock, I'll be gone."

"I'll be here."

Daniel nodded, took up the reins, and guided the wagon down the gravel driveway. Johanna watched him leave and wished she were already on the way.

She hurried to join Cecile. She could feel her heart beating against her chest. *What am I doing? I'll get caught. I'll be convicted of kidnapping. Locked up in jail or thrown out of Hamburg. No help for Rebecca. No help for Mama.*

"Why were you talking to the driver?" asked Cecile.

"I needed to ask him something."

"What?"

"About … about Altona."

"Altona? You could ask *me* about Altona!"

"All right," said Johanna. "What's it like?"

"It's a small town," Cecile said. "You can almost spit from Hamburg to Altona. After all, they're only about two and a half miles apart."

"I know that. But what is Altona *like*?"

Cecile linked her arm into Johanna's. The two made their way to the kitchen for breakfast. "It's a lot like Hamburg. On the main street, there are shops and houses and people coming and going. There's ice in the winter and mud the rest of the time and stink all the time."

While they were eating, Johanna tried to find out more about Altona. "If a person were in Altona," Johanna asked, "how would he get to Amsterdam?"

Cecile answered between chews. "By wagon or coach, I suppose. Or, if you had money, you could travel by ship."

"Is there any other way to get there?"

"Sure. You could fly like a bird!"

"Very funny! As if people can fly!"

"Why are you asking all those questions?" Monica demanded.

"I just wanted to know. One day, I'd like to go to Amsterdam," Johanna said.

"What would *you* do there?" Monica said.

"I could sell my lace work," Johanna said. "Or even become a governess."

"You?" Monica snorted. "An upper-class family would never hire you."

"I've heard that Amsterdam is a beautiful city," Cecile said, putting a hand on Johanna's arm.

"There's only one problem," Monica said.

"What?" said Johanna.

Monica sneered. "They let Jews become citizens."

The next evening was Friday. Johanna sat alone in her room. She fingered Mama's lace kerchief. Since she had come to the orphanage, she hadn't dared light Sabbath candles. But tonight she felt lonely. She yearned for the glow of the candles.

She put two candles in candlesticks on the table, placed the kerchief on her head, lit the candles, and began to recite the blessing. "*Baruch atah adonei eloheynu —*"

Someone was knocking on the door. Johanna's heart skipped a beat. "Who is it?"

"It's me."

"Cecile?"

"May I come in?"

"Just a minute!" Johanna shoved the kerchief under her pillow and opened the door.

"What took so long?" Cecile asked. She gazed at the candles flickering in the dimness. "Those candlesticks are beautiful. Where did you get them?"

"I … I borrowed them from … Frau Hartmann."

"You did? Why?"

"I … I misplaced mine."

"I see." Cecile looked puzzled.

"Did you want something?"

Cecile looked about the room. She seemed to have forgotten why she'd come. "Oh, can I borrow a needle and thread?"

"Of course." Johanna rummaged in the top drawer of her dresser. "Here," she said, handing the notions to Cecile.

"Thank you. Have a good night."

"You too." Johanna's heart was pounding and her fingers trembled. *Has Cecile guessed my secret? Some non-Jews know about Sabbath candles. Will she tell Frau Taubman before I escape? I'll have to leave the orphanage. I won't be able to rescue Rebecca. And if I don't, she will surely die.*

Chapter Six

An Unexpected Companion

On Sunday, Johanna wore her shawl to the nursery. When no one was looking, she stuffed clothes and diapers into the shawl. Later that night, she stole bread and cheese from the kitchen, as well as a small jug of milk for Rebecca.

Her hands shook; her legs trembled. She had an uneasy feeling that she was being followed on the way back to her room. She kept looking behind her, imagining that someone was standing in the shadows, watching her.

Early Monday morning, Johanna put a few last items into her bag and fastened it tightly. She wrapped her cloak around her shoulders, tied her hat on her head, and put on her shoes.

Johanna took one last look around her little room. *I came here with such hope. Now all I feel is sadness about the past and worry for the future.* She sighed, straightened her back, and closed the door softly behind her.

She walked down the steep narrow stairs and along a corridor. Weak sunlight sifted in through the windows. She heard the clatter of pots and pans in the kitchen and smelled freshly baked bread and porridge simmering on the stove. She heard Frau Hartmann humming an old country tune.

For a moment, she wished she could join the other girls and forget her plan. One step into the kitchen, and she would be safe. One step away led to an unknown future. She felt paralyzed with uncertainty.

Then she remembered the babies who had died, their stiff grey corpses wrapped in coarse linen, carted away to unmarked graves. She shuddered and began to walk towards the nursery.

"Johanna," someone whispered.

"Who is it?" Johanna asked, her heart pounding. She turned towards the voice. A dark shape was standing in the shadow of a doorway.

"It's me."

"Who?"

"Me! Cecile." She wore her cloak and hat, and clutched a bag in her hands.

"What are you doing here?" Johanna asked.

"I know what you're planning."

"What are you talking about?"

"You've been planning to run away for days now. I saw you," Cecile said. "I saw you take some food from the kitchen. And you were asking about Altona —"

Johanna shook her head. "I have to go. We'll talk about it tomorrow."

Cecile took a step towards Johanna. "Not likely. You'll be gone by tomorrow."

"But —"

"You're running away." Cecile took another step towards her and grabbed her arm. "And I want to go with you."

Johanna shrugged off Cecile's hand. "So, I'm leaving," she said. "That doesn't mean you can come with me." More gently, she added, "Besides, we can't both leave at the same time!"

Cecile pursed her lips as she peered along the corridor. "I don't care. All I know is that I must leave this horrid place. And I must leave today!"

"Cecile, you don't understand," said Johanna. She turned to face Cecile and put her hands on her friend's shoulders. "I'm not going alone. I'm taking one of my babies with me."

"Are you crazy?"

"I can't ... I *won't* watch another baby die."

"Do you know what will happen if they catch you? They'll throw you in jail! Or worse!" Cecile paused. "Which one?"

"Which what?"

"Which *baby*? I'm not talking about apples!"

Johanna pushed past Cecile. Time was growing short. She was afraid Daniel would leave without her. "I have to go!"

"Please, Johanna!" Cecile cried after her. "Please let me come with you!" Johanna looked back at Cecile.

"You're willing to give up this job?"

"I don't care," Cecile said. "I haven't heard from my family for weeks. I'm afraid to go alone. I won't be in your way and ... maybe I can help."

What if I don't let her come? Johanna thought. *Will she betray me?* "All right. You may come with me as far as Altona."

"Great!" She grabbed Johanna by the arm. "Let's go!"

"Be quiet! They'll hear you."

"Sorry."

"Meet me outside, behind the hedge near the road," said Johanna. "I'll go get Rebecca."

"Wait," Cecile said. "Give me your bag. You'll have to carry the baby." She grinned. "See? I'm already a help!"

In the nursery, one girl was dozing in a chair; two others were playing a game of checkers, out of sight of the babies. The babies were sleeping, or lying listlessly in their beds.

Johanna tiptoed over to Rebecca's bed. Rebecca was deep in dreams, her tiny mouth twitching slightly. Johanna picked her up. She felt her warmth against her chest. Just then, one of the girls said, "Johanna, where are you taking that baby?"

Johanna froze in her tracks. She felt her heart racing and could scarcely speak. "Keller ... Doctor Keller asked me to bring her to him."

"Oh? I didn't know he was here."

"He ... came by hired carriage." Rebecca was reaching towards Johanna's face and playing with her hair. "I must go. The doctor doesn't like to be kept waiting."

"All right, but —"

"Lise," the other girl whispered, "It's your turn." Lise shrugged and turned back to the game.

Johanna wrapped her cloak around Rebecca, hurried out of the room, and closed the door behind her. Her heart pounding, she whispered the words of a psalm she remembered from home:

> *The help of the innocent comes*
> *from the Lord.*
> *Their strength is He in time of need.*
> *The Lord helps them and rescues them.*
> *He rescues them from the wicked*
> *and saves them,*
> *Because they trust in Him.*

The words carried her along the corridor, through the grand foyer, and out the front door.

What have I done? Johanna thought. *How will I travel on the dangerous road to Amsterdam with a nine-month-old baby?* Her fear was almost more than she could bear. She stood frozen on the front step.

A man came hurrying up the path. When he reached Johanna, he stopped and said, "Why, it is Fraulein … Richter, is it not?"

"Yes," mumbled Johanna, curtseying. "We met at my interview."

"Quite right," said Herr Vogel. He looked down at the squirming bundle in Johanna's arms. "Where, may I ask, are you going with that baby?"

"I … I'm taking her outside for some fresh air."

"I see." Herr Vogel paused. "Nowhere else?"

"No," said Johanna, blushing. "Where else would I take her?" *Another lie*, she thought. *I am getting quite skillful at that particular sin.*

Herr Vogel peered over Johanna's shoulder. "If I were taking care of these babies …" He pursed his lips. "… these *dying* babies who are subject to an experiment …"

"Yes?" said Johanna. "What would you do?"

Herr Vogel averted his eyes. "I might want to rescue one of the babies."

"You would?" Johanna's heart skipped a beat. *Does Herr Vogel suspect what I am doing? Will he betray me?*

"I am not saying I *would*." Herr Vogel raised his eyebrows. "Only that I *might* want to." He lowered his eyebrows. "But of course, the risks would be great; the punishment, severe. Still …"

"Still?"

"A human life." Herr Vogel put his hand on Johanna's arm. "Worth the risk, I believe." He looked straight at Johanna, as if he could read her mind. "And if I were to take that risk, I would leave as quickly as possible." He sighed and took out his pocket watch. "I must go now. I have an appointment with a certain Frau Taubman." As he turned to go, he said. "Fraulein Richter?"

"Yes?" Johanna's knees were shaking.

"Godspeed."

"Thank you, sir."

Johanna looked down into Rebecca's trusting eyes. The baby smiled up at her.

"I'll do it," whispered Johanna. "It is a matter of life and death. Your life, and mine, too, if it is to have any meaning."

Johanna looked up and saw Cecile peeking out from behind the hedge. Johanna straightened her back and strode towards her waiting companion.

The sun was shining in a sky of watery blue. A brisk wind whipped her cloak about and tried to lift her long skirt. It dried the tears in her eyes — tears she hadn't been aware of.

"What happened?" said Cecile. "I thought you would never come!"

"I'll tell you later. Let's find Daniel."

They heard Daniel before they saw him. Snores rumbled from his throat. His cap was pulled over his eyes and his whiskered chin was resting on his chest. The reins lay slack in his hands. An empty jug of beer lay next to him on the wagon seat.

"Wait here," Johanna whispered. "I'll talk to Daniel." She walked over to Daniel and shook his arm. "Wake up!" The snoring only grew louder. She shook his arm again. "Daniel, wake up!" But no matter how hard Johanna shook him, he wouldn't respond.

She gestured for Cecile to join her. "We have a little problem."

Cecile's eyes opened wide. "What's the matter?"

"Our driver is ... slightly inebriated."

"You mean drunk?"

"Right." Johanna frowned. "He must have been drinking all night long."

"What do we do now?"

"You don't happen to know how to drive a wagon, do you?" said Johanna.

Cecile grinned. "As a matter of fact, I do."

"Wait. Don't tell me," said Johanna, holding up her hand. "Your brother showed you how."

Cecile shrugged. "He taught me almost everything I know."

———◆———

They'd gone only a short distance when Daniel woke up. "What's going on here?" he said. He snatched the reins from Cecile and pulled hard to stop the wagon. "Who are you? What're you doing driving my wagon?"

"Uh, Daniel," said Johanna. "There's been a little … change of plans."

"I asked you and you'd better answer quick. Who *is* she?" Daniel reached for the jug. "If you're trying to get me into trouble …"

"She's Cecile. My … my friend. She's coming, too."

"And who says I'll take her?"

"Please, Daniel," Johanna said.

Daniel looked sideways at the two girls. "What's in it for me? Ain't I taking enough risks already?" He brought the jug to his lips. "Agh! Empty!" He plunked the jug down on the floor under the seat.

Johanna looked hard at Cecile and said, "She'll pay you, too. Right, Cecile?"

"Of course I'll pay," Cecile said. She looked at Johanna. "How much?"

"You should be asking *me*, not her!" Daniel said, pointing to his chest.

"Sorry. How much, sir?" Cecile said.

"That's more like it." He paused. "Tell you what. I'll make you a deal. Only ten schillings for you." He glanced at Johanna. "Less risk. Pay five now, five when we get to Altona." Cecile counted the schillings into Daniel's hand. He turned towards Johanna. "Now you."

Johanna put nine schillings into Daniel's hand. She smelled onions, garlic, and some other unidentifiable odour. He stuffed the coins in his pocket.

"Now let's get out of here," Daniel said.

Chapter Seven

Plague

Daniel guided the wagon to the Hafenstrasse, which ran west along the waterfront towards Altona. The sounds of a new day filled Johanna's ears: the grinding of wagon wheels and the clip-clop of the horse's hooves, the screaming of gulls and the chiming of the town clock.

The girls sat huddled together on a blanket in the back of the wagon. They bumped against the sides of the wagon and against each other until they soon felt bruised and irritable.

Rebecca woke up and began crying. Johanna gave her a piece of bread, but the baby pushed it away. She squirmed and whined in Johanna's arms. She felt heavier and heavier as they proceeded on the road.

Daniel was muttering to himself, occasionally glancing back at the girls. After some time had passed, he stopped the wagon in front of an inn.

The wooden walls were rotting; the roof was missing shingles. The sound of laughter and shouting wafted out of the open windows and into the street.

"Wait here," Daniel said. "I'm going in to wet my throat a bit."

"Please don't stop," said Johanna. "We need to get as far away from the orphanage as we can."

"I'm the driver," Daniel said. "You'll do as I say." He smiled, showing several gaps in his teeth. "Unless you want to walk." He got down from the wagon, tied the reins to a post near the horse trough, and staggered into the inn.

Johanna sighed and opened her bag. "I wanted to leave right away, so I didn't eat anything today. This seems as good a time as any." She put Rebecca down on a blanket and handed her a piece of cheese. Rebecca grabbed it and clutched it in her fist.

"Here," Johanna said, handing Cecile a piece of bread and cheese.

"Thank you," said Cecile. "I'm starving!" She looked back down the road towards Hamburg. "Johanna, do you think we're being followed?"

Johanna shrugged. "I can't be sure. All I know is I'm doing what I have to do."

"I wish I could have taken one of *my* babies, too."

"If you want to leave, then leave," Johanna snapped. "Go into the inn, and ask someone to take you back. Or go wherever you want to go." All the tension and sleepless nights had caught up with Johanna. She felt tired to her very bones. More gently, she added, "I won't blame you."

"I'm not leaving," Cecile said, jutting out her chin. "I'm going to Altona with you."

Johanna squeezed Cecile's arm. "I was hoping you'd say that. And Cecile?"

"What?"

"I'm sorry I was rude just now. I'm wound up like a spring."

"It's all right," Cecile said. "A few words aren't going to spoil our friendship."

Johanna smiled wanly. "I hope not."

"That's better," Daniel said, coming out of the inn and wiping his mouth with his sleeve. He untied the reins, climbed back onto the wagon, and snapped the horse's reins.

Approaching Altona, they passed a wagon leaving the town. The wagon driver had a cloth pulled tightly around his nose and mouth. He pointed behind him, in the direction of Altona.

"If you know what's good for you, don't go there," he said.

"What's that?" said Daniel.

The man shuddered. "Plague!"

Daniel pulled hard on the reins, as if the wagon were about to fall off a cliff. Cecile covered her face with a corner of her cloak. Johanna pulled Rebecca closer to her chest. Johanna looked behind her as the other wagon moved away. Corpses two and three deep were piled haphazardly on it. The bodies shook with every jolt of the wagon.

Everyone knew about the plagues that had spread throughout Europe over the years. Johanna didn't know all the names of the plague the physicians used. All she knew was that plague was usually fatal.

If one person in a family caught the plague, the entire family would be locked inside their house. Watchmen would check the house from time to time to make sure no one tried to leave. The family would all be dead within the space of a week. Then the gravediggers would come to pile their carts with the sad cargoes and bring them to the cemeteries.

Rich or poor, good or bad — the plague didn't discriminate. It killed almost everyone it found, wiping out entire families and communities.

When the cemeteries were full, when the mounds of earth created unnatural hills two or three feet high, the dead would be carted to the country to be buried in huge open pits. There was no time for a decent burial; no time for the bereaved to mourn. It was often their turn to die next.

"I'm not going any closer!" said Daniel.

"I must see if my family has been spared," Cecile said.

"Forget it," said Daniel, shaking his head. "I'm not going into a plague-infested town." He held the reins tightly. "I kept my part of the bargain. Don't say I didn't. But I'm not going there!"

"Please!" Cecile said.

"I can't and I won't," said Daniel. "I've lost enough of my own family to the plague." He gestured with his thumb. "Now get off!"

Should I go with Cecile? Johanna thought. *How much do I dare risk? My life, and Rebecca's as well?* She squared her shoulders, took a deep breath, and looked into Cecile's eyes. *She's my friend. I must help her.*

"Come, Cecile. I'll go with you," Johanna said. "But first we must pay Daniel."

Daniel held out his dirty hand. The girls reached into their meagre purses and paid him the schillings they owed him.

The girls got down from the wagon. Cecile clutched their bags and Johanna held tightly to the baby. Johanna now understood what people meant when they talked about a heavy heart. Hers felt like lead. Her thoughts whirled about her head as they began to walk away. But then she had an idea.

"Daniel!" she shouted, hurrying after the wagon. "Wait!"

Daniel pulled the reins up sharply. "What now?"

"Will you do something for us?"

Daniel glanced back towards Altona. "Depends what."

"Wait for us here? At least," she whispered, "at least until we know what happened to Cecile's family." She paused. "And please watch the baby. She's sleeping. She won't be any trouble."

"That's asking a lot," Daniel said.

"We'll come back as soon as we can. I promise."

"I don't know much about babies." He took off his cap and wiped the sweat on his forehead with the back of his arm.

"I promise we'll be back within the hour."

"All right," said Daniel, nodding. "I'll watch her, but for Christ's sake, cover your nose and mouth!"

Johanna and Cecile plodded along the rutted road. No laundry hung on clotheslines. No children played in the streets. The few people hurrying by kept their faces covered and their heads down.

Scrawny cats prowled in the lanes. Piles of rotting garbage were piled on the streets, in alleys, in front of houses and shops. The stench of rotten food and open sewers filled the air. Johanna stopped and vomited until her stomach was empty, leaving a sour taste in her mouth.

They made their way to the town square where a ragged throng of people crowded around the church. Several people were beating on the heavy wooden doors with their fists.

"For mercy's sake!" cried a scarecrow of a man. "Let us in!"

"The rich bastards," muttered another. "They ran away and left us here to rot!"

"And now the church won't even let us in!" wailed a woman.

A narrow window beside the door slid open. A man wearing a black hood stuck his head out. "Go away! You cannot come in," the minister croaked. "May God help you all. Now, go away!" He slammed the window shut.

"God has surely abandoned us!" a woman cried. The crowd dispersed. Their cries and moans were carried away in the foul air.

Johanna and Cecile continued on their weary way among the dead and the dying. The air was filled with the moans of the suffering and the wails of the bereaved.

A child, not more than three years old, sat beside the body of a woman on the side of the road. "Mama! Mama! Up Mama!" he cried. His mother did not answer. She was dead.

Further along the street, a man and woman lay together, stiff in a last macabre embrace. Flies buzzed around their eyes and noses.

A man sat on the ground, his back to a building. His face and neck was a mass of sores oozing pus. "For pity's sake!" he wheezed. "Water!"

Cecile pointed to a small white house and cried, "There it is!"

No smoke wafted up through the chimney. Pale geraniums sat wilting in their window boxes. The front door had been nailed shut with a broad piece of wood. Someone had painted a large red cross on the door.

A sign was tacked on the door. "What does it say?" Cecile whispered.

Johanna's voice trembled as she read the scrawled black words:

PLAGUE HOUSE.

IT IS FORBIDDEN TO ENTER

OR LEAVE THESE PREMISES.

MAY GOD HAVE MERCY ON US ALL.
— TOWN COUNCIL OF ALTONA

Cecile gasped and went rigid, as if turned to stone. Then she began to sob, her body shaking uncontrollably. "This must be why … I haven't heard from them … all this time."

Johanna held Cecile for a long time, until at last her sobbing lessened.

"Cecile, we must go." Cecile shuddered. "There is nothing we can do here. And if we stay, we might catch the plague."

"Wait! Antoine and I used to have a hiding place!" Cecile broke away from Johanna and stumbled forward. She lifted an odd-shaped rock near the entrance to the house and picked up a piece of folded paper. With shaking fingers, she handed the paper to Johanna. "Read this," she ordered.

Johanna took the paper from Cecile and read aloud, "*Dearest Cecile, I am well. I escaped the plague. I've written you several letters, but they were all returned unopened….*"

"Frau Taubman!" Cecile cried. "She probably heard about the plague here and knew I'd leave right away if I found out."

"Probably. Here, let me finish." Johanna turned back to the letter. "*I am going to Bremen to stay with friends at Kolpingstrasse, Number 17. Send word when you can. God keep you safe. In haste, your loving brother, Antoine. P.S. Please thank whoever reads you this letter from the bottom of my heart.*"

Johanna handed the paper back to Cecile, who clutched it to her chest. "I must go there," she gasped. "To Bremen. To Antoine."

Johanna's heart sank. But when she looked at her grief-stricken friend, she knew what she must do. "We will go there together," Johanna said.

"You'll go with me?"

Johanna nodded. "Of course I will." They hurried back to where they had left Daniel and the sleeping baby.

"It's about time you got back," Daniel said. "I'm not cut out to be a nursemaid."

Johanna looked at the unkempt driver and smiled for the first time that day. "No indeed," she said. "You are not." She took Rebecca from Daniel and kissed her gently on the head. Then she climbed into the wagon.

Daniel snapped the reins before they had scarcely sat down.

"What now?" he asked, as he forced the horse into a quick trot.

"We need to go to Bremen," Johanna said. "Will you take us?"

"Bremen? That's another day's journey," said Daniel. "Forget it!"

"But we have no other way," said Johanna.

"I must go there. To my brother."

Daniel shook his head. "You paid me to take you to Altona. That's all."

Johanna swallowed hard. "We'll pay you extra to take us. Won't we, Cecile?"

Cecile looked sullen, but then nodded.

Daniel stared at the two young women, and then at the sleeping baby in Johanna's arms. "That's a dangerous road, full of robbers and low-lifes." He scratched his head and wiped his nose on his dirty sleeve. Then he sighed. "I guess I can take you there."

Johanna was so relieved she could barely speak. "Thank you, Daniel. I don't know what to say."

"There's nothing to say," Daniel replied. "Now let's get out of this cursed town!"

Chapter Eight

A Chance Meeting

Whether it was due to the dryness of his throat or the dusty road or the monotony of the voyage, Daniel soon revealed just how insatiable his thirst for beer was. Every hour or so, he stopped the wagon and went into an alehouse. Each time he returned, his step was more unsteady, his breath stronger, his nose redder.

Cecile was consumed by grief, and said not a word. Rebecca woke up cranky, whining and squirming about. Johanna tried to comfort her, but wondered if Rebecca sensed her own nervousness.

Johanna was tormented by worry about what lay ahead, about what would happen to Mama, and whether she had made the right decision. *Perhaps I should turn back. Perhaps it is not too late.* But with every mile they travelled away from Hamburg, Johanna knew it was indeed too late to go back. *No. I have begun this journey and I must see it to its end.*

By late afternoon, Johanna could contain herself no longer. "Daniel, that is enough. If we don't stop at an inn soon, you can … give us back our money. Or …"

"Or what?" Daniel snarled. "Are you threatening me, girl? What are you going to do, eh? Walk back to Hamburg? Or maybe go to the police and tell them you kidnapped a baby?"

Johanna smiled wanly. "I'm not threatening you. Do I look as if I could?"

"Not likely!"

"Only … we need to stop soon." She looked up and down the road. "Most travellers have already stopped for the night. And you said it was dangerous …."

"You've got a point there," Daniel said as he scratched his armpit. "All right. We'll stop at the next town."

When they reached the town of Elsdorf, Daniel finally stopped at an inn. The girls clambered from the wagon and followed Daniel inside. A fire crackled in the large brick fireplace at one end of the large room. Candles flickered in brass sconces on the walls. A motley group of travellers were seated on benches set around tables. The air was thick with the smell of unwashed bodies, sour beer, warmed-over cabbage, and stale tobacco smoke.

"Innkeeper!" Daniel shouted. "Service here!"

A slight, nervous-looking man came up to them. His red hair stuck up on top of his head. He wiped his hands on a dirty cloth hanging from his waist. His smile revealed that most of his teeth were missing. "Of course, of course, come right in."

He showed them to a stained wooden table, which he wiped hastily with his cloth. "A lick and a promise, a lick and a promise." He looked at Daniel and the girls. "Make yourselves comfortable. Always nice to welcome travellers, I say. Name's Schmidt. At your service," he added, making a small bow. "At your service."

They sat down on the benches on either side of the table.

"Will you be staying the night?" Schmidt asked. "I have a nice room for you. A nice room."

"Yes," said Johanna. "We'll need a room for us women and the baby."

"That's fine. That's fine," said Schmidt, rubbing his hands together. "We have a nice stew with dumplings tonight. It'll stick to your ribs, stick to your ribs."

"Some beer first, then that stew," Daniel said.

"Please bring a cup of warm milk for the baby," Johanna said. Rebecca was squirming beneath her cloak. Johanna glanced at Cecile, who looked pale and worn out.

"Right away, right away," said Schmidt as he hurried away.

A few minutes later, a young girl brought a pitcher of beer and three pewter mugs to the table, as well as a steaming cup of milk.

Daniel gulped his beer greedily. "There," he said, wiping his mouth, "That's better." He refilled his mug, downed the contents, and said, "Be right back. Call of nature." He walked unsteadily out a door at the back of the inn.

Johanna put Rebecca on her lap and helped her drink the warm milk. The baby gulped eagerly, giving little sighs of contentment between each swallow. Johanna sipped her beer and gazed around the room.

In a dark corner, she noticed a man who was sitting alone. The curls in his long wig and the spotless lace at his cuffs gleamed in the candlelight. *He must be important. He is sitting on a fancy chair with carved legs, not on a plain bench like everyone else.*

"Cecile, look over there," Johanna whispered, tilting her head towards the man.

"Where?"

"In the corner. Who is that man? Doesn't he look familiar?"

"I can't see. It's too dark."

At that moment, the man rose from his chair and walked towards their table. Johanna gasped. It was Herr Vogel, the duke's secretary! *How did he find us? What should I do?* She turned away and quickly covered Rebecca with her cloak.

"Excuse me," Vogel said, tipping his hat. "It is wonderful to see you again so soon, Fraulein Richter." He glanced at Cecile. "And you are Fraulein Hansen, if I am not mistaken?"

Johanna's heart was beating so loudly she was sure even Daniel could hear it from wherever he had gone. *How did he find us? Has he been ordered to bring us back? Or take us to the police?*

"We have just come from Altona," said Johanna. She kicked Cecile's foot under the table.

Cecile grimaced. "Yes," she said. "To visit my family."

"Ah, now I remember. You are from Altona. But I heard there is plague there." He paused. "May I sit down?"

Johanna nodded and gestured to the bench.

Cecile swallowed hard and her eyes filled with tears.

"Why, what is the matter?" Vogel asked.

"Nothing," Cecile said.

Rebecca began to squirm and poked her head from under the cloak. She gazed from one person to another, as if listening to the conversation.

"Cecile is … disappointed … because we decided not to go to Altona after all," Johanna said. Her armpits were wet and the sweat was running down her back. "That's why we stopped here. At this inn. Before going back to the orphanage." *I'm becoming an expert liar. What would Mama say?*

Vogel cleared his throat. "What a coincidence we met," he said. "I am on the road. Business for the duke." Vogel glanced down at the baby, opened his mouth to speak, but stopped himself. He had a thoughtful look on his face. "I wish you a pleasant journey," he said, standing up. "I shall leave you alone now. You must be weary."

"Thank you," Johanna managed to say.

Vogel tipped his hat and returned to his seat.

The girls didn't speak. They looked at each other, the worry plain on their faces.

"That's better," said Daniel as he sat down across from the girls a moment later.

Schmidt carried a large tray to their table. "Here you are now. Here's your supper. The best stew in the country, made fresh today. Fresh today. Eat up, eat up."

"Herr Schmidt, may I wash my hands somewhere?" Johanna asked. She always tried to wash her hands before eating. It was a habit from home she didn't want to break.

"Wash your hands?" he said. "What a strange request." Johanna could feel her face growing red. She looked down to avoid his eyes.

"Go out back to the kitchen. My wife will show you where."

"Cecile?" Johanna said. Cecile seemed lost in her own world. "Cecile," Johanna repeated, shaking her friend's shoulder.

"What?" Cecile looked at Johanna with red-rimmed eyes.

"Please hold Rebecca while I'm gone." Johanna placed the squirming baby into Cecile's stiff arms. "I'll be right back."

Rebecca began to cry. Her crying tugged at a deep place in Johanna's heart.

"I'll take her," Daniel said. "She seems to like me."

Johanna hurried to the kitchen, where Frau Schmidt gave her a basin of water to wash her hands. Her legs were shaking. *Should we leave the inn while we have the chance? Perhaps Vogel will call the police. Perhaps we'll be thrown into jail.* They had been gone only one day, but already the journey seemed endless.

"Please God," she whispered, as she splashed water on her face. "Please keep us safe."

When she returned to the main room, she glanced over to the corner where Herr Vogel had been sitting. He was gone.

Chapter Nine

A Sleepless Night

Herr Schmidt led the girls to a dingy room above the inn. He left hastily and said, "Good night. Good night."

Cecile collapsed on the bed and was soon fast asleep. Johanna's arms and legs felt heavy with fatigue, but she forced herself to change Rebecca's diaper and wash her hands and face. She held Rebecca's hands and clapped them together while she sang a children's song she remembered from home:

> *Clap, clap your little hands.*
> *Papa will buy you little shoes.*
> *Mama will knit you a little shirt.*
> *And you will have rosy cheeks.*

Rebecca began to cry and thrashed about in Johanna's arms. Johanna walked back and forth in the cramped room and tried to comfort the baby. She hummed a lullaby over and over, until at last Rebecca fell asleep, her head resting on Johanna's shoulder. She put Rebecca in a small bed in a corner of the room and lay down beside Cecile, who was already snoring loudly.

Johanna couldn't get comfortable. Cecile kicked her legs about in all directions, rolled over, and yanked the blanket from Johanna. She lay shivering beside Cecile for what seemed like an endless night. Her worries kept turning around in her head. *Are we being followed? How can I protect Rebecca? How can I tell Mama what I've done and where I'm going?*

Finally, just as she was falling into an exhausted sleep, Rebecca began to cry. Johanna dragged herself out of bed and lit a candle. She changed Rebecca's diaper and walked back and forth with her, until at last Rebecca fell asleep again. Johanna lay down with Rebecca in her arms. She lay awake until at last she saw daylight peeping in through the cracks of the shutters.

Her mouth tasted of stale beer; her stomach was making rumbling noises from last night's stew. Her clothes were starting to smell and so was her body. Her head was pounding and her eyes were sore. When she'd originally planned to run away, she hadn't imagined that she would feel so tired and dirty after just one day.

And now Rebecca had a rash spreading from her neck down to her stomach. Johanna shook Cecile on the shoulder. "Wake up!" she said.

"What?" Cecile yawned. "Is it morning already?"

"Rebecca is sick."

"Sick?" Cecile sat bolt upright and pulled Rebecca's nightgown up over her stomach. "She's got a rash."

Johanna swallowed hard. "I know. But what kind of rash?"

"How should I know? Do I look like Doctor Keller?"

The thought of Cecile looking anything like the rotund Doctor Keller made both girls grin. "Not even close!"

Cecile pointed to Rebecca's stomach. "It looks like the kind of rash children get. Not —"

"Plague," whispered Johanna.

"No, I don't think so," said Cecile, shuddering.

"Perhaps it will clear up by itself."

"You should take her to a doctor as soon as you can."

Johanna nodded. She knew she must, but a doctor's fees would take more money from her already thin purse. "Please don't say anything to anyone," she said.

"I won't."

Someone was knocking on the door.

"Yes?" Both girls answered at the same time.

"I've brought some water for washing," a girl said from the other side of the door.

"Come in," Johanna said.

The young girl who had served them the previous night entered the room. Her hair was dishevelled under her cap; her dress and apron were the same ones she had worn the day before. She emptied the dirty water from the basin and the contents of the chamber pot into a bucket. Then she poured warm water from a kettle she was carrying into the basin.

The girl glanced at Rebecca. "What's wrong with your baby?"

"Nothing," Johanna snapped. "Just a rash."

The girl gasped and brought her hand to her mouth. "A rash? That's how plague starts!" She grabbed the bucket and backed away. Her chest rose and fell quickly; she eyed the baby nervously. She left the door open behind her in her haste to get away.

"We have to get out of here!" Cecile whispered.

Johanna groaned. "All right. But I want to wash the baby first."

Johanna put Rebecca in the basin and gave her a sponge bath. "Maybe this will help her feel better," Johanna said. But Rebecca lay in the water, her eyes dull, and her body listless.

"My mother used to say —" Cecile said.

"Yes?" Johanna tried to keep hold of the slippery baby.

"— that too many baths makes a person sick."

"Well, *my* mother doesn't think so," Johanna said. She dried the baby and put the last clean diaper on her bottom. "It is just superstition that makes people not want to wash." She sighed. Her head felt as if it were stuffed with wool. "In my religion, you're supposed to wash a lot."

"What do you mean, 'my religion'?"

"Nothing." Johanna could feel her face getting red. She wished she could take back what she'd said.

Cecile stood with crossed arms and glared at Johanna. "Aren't you Lutheran like me?" She shuddered. "Or are you one of those papist Catholics?"

Johanna shook her head. The baby was squirming in her arms.

"If you're not Lutheran or Catholic, what *are* you?" said Cecile.

Johanna took a big breath. "I'm Jewish."

"You're *what*?" Cecile took a few steps back and sat down on the bed, hard.

"I'm Jewish."

"Oh." Cecile's voice had grown cold. "I see."

"Does it make a difference? We're still friends, aren't we?"

Cecile's eyes darted about the room. She refused to look at Johanna. "I don't know. I've never met anyone who was Jewish." She shuddered. "You killed Christ. Everyone knows that."

"Look at me, Cecile!" Johanna said. She sat down beside Cecile, who turned her back to her. "I'm still the same person you've known for months. I haven't suddenly changed just because you know that I'm Jewish."

"Maybe ..." said Cecile. "But I heard the plague is all your fault."

"Mine?"

"No, not *yours*. You know, the Jews' fault."

"That's ridiculous!"

"Then why don't you Jews get the plague?"

"We *do*." Johanna paused. "My grandfather had the plague. He died of it. So did my sister and brother."

"Oh," said Cecile. "I didn't know."

Johanna reached over and touched Cecile's hand.

"Don't touch me!" Cecile cried, pulling away. "Even if that's true, you've been lying to me all these months!" She stood up and paced the floor. "You didn't trust me to keep your precious secret!" she hissed. "So maybe now I won't!"

Cecile stuffed her belongings into her bag and walked towards the door. "I'm going to tell Daniel. I'm sure he won't want to take a lying *Jew* anywhere!"

"Wait, Cecile! I can explain!" But Cecile had slammed the door behind her and was already hurrying down the stairs.

The baby began to cry. With shaking hands, Johanna held her close and walked with her as she sang Mama's lullaby.

> *Sleep, little baby, safely sleep.*
> *The birds are singing in the woods.*
> *They sing and hop in the grass so green.*
> *They'll bring the baby something good.*

Johanna walked and sang, walked and sang, until at last Rebecca quieted down. Johanna dressed her, and put her on the floor gently. She washed the diapers in the tepid water. *What will Cecile do now?* Johanna's heart was beating wildly in her chest. *Will she tell Daniel? Will he hate me now, too? Will he go to Bremen without me and leave me here alone?*

She gathered her things and shoved them into her bag. She picked Rebecca up in one arm, her bag and the bundle of wet diapers in the other. She pushed the door open with her hip and made her way down the narrow stairs to the main room of the inn.

Cecile glared at Johanna as she walked into the room. When Johanna sat down beside her on the bench, Cecile slid away.

"I thought you were going to sleep all day," said Daniel, as he looked up from his bowl of porridge. Stray pieces of straw poked out of his hair. "Sit down. Have some breakfast." He motioned at her with his spoon.

"I'm not very hungry," said Johanna, "but maybe something for the baby." She glanced at Cecile. "Did she …?"

"Listen here," said Daniel, waving his spoon. "Makes no difference to me if you eat or not. Or what religion you are." He wiped his mouth on his sleeve. "Lutheran, Catholic, Jew, Turk, whatever — as long as you pay me."

Johanna let out her breath. She nodded but couldn't speak.

Herr Schmidt came up to their table. "How did you sleep? Like a log, like a log, I hope," he said, rubbing his hands together.

"Yes," said Cecile.

"No," said Johanna at the same time.

"You'll be wanting some breakfast," said Schmidt. He turned towards the kitchen and called,

"Katrina! Some breakfast for our guests here. Be quick about it!"

The girl brought porridge, milk, and bread to the table. She almost spilled everything several times. She did everything she could to avoid coming close to Johanna and the baby. After she had served them, she sidled over to Schmidt and whispered in his ear. He frowned and walked over to their table.

"What's this Katrina tells me?" Schmidt stood over them, his hands on his hips.

"What do you mean?" asked Johanna, stalling for time.

"Why didn't you tell me the baby's sick?" Schmidt stepped back. "Didn't you say you came from Altona?" He narrowed his eyes. "I heard there's plague there."

"What if we did?" said Daniel. He picked up the knife and passed it from one hand to the other.

"You should have told me."

"You didn't ask," said Daniel.

"Let us eat something first, then we'll be on our way," said Johanna.

"Well ... I don't know," said Schmidt.

"We'll leave soon," said Daniel, still handling the knife. "Just let them have their breakfast."

"All right. All right," said Schmidt. "Eat up and then I want you gone."

"Thank you," said Johanna.

"Nothing but trouble," Schmidt muttered as he walked away. "Nothing but trouble." Daniel placed the knife on the table.

Johanna gulped down the lukewarm porridge while she fed Rebecca. The baby kept grabbing the bowl and spoon out of her hand.

"We should get to Bremen by the end of the day," Daniel said, chewing with his mouth open. "And that's where I'll be leaving you." He gulped the last of his coffee and stood up. "Time to go."

"All right," Johanna said. "To Bremen it is." *From there, I must find a way to reach Amsterdam.*

"Are you done yet?" Schmidt said. "Time to pay and leave."

"Thank you, Herr Schmidt," said Johanna. "We are." She counted out a few coins. He pointed to the table, where she put them down.

"Be gone with you," Schmidt said, gesturing towards the door. "Be gone with you."

Chapter Ten

An Unpleasant Encounter

The horse plodded along the rutted road towards Bremen. Solitary trees and small farmhouses occasionally broke the monotony of the flat land. Farmers ploughed their fields; cows and sheep grazed in the pastures. Johanna missed the city, the people hurrying to and fro on the busy streets. But most of all, she missed Mama. Her homesickness had become a physical ache. *I wanted to see the world. Now all I want is to go home.* She sighed. *But I began this journey, and now I must finish it.*

As the wagon jolted along, Johanna felt more bruises added to the ones she'd gotten the day before. Daniel stopped several times to pee in the bushes by the side of the road. He kept muttering things like, "I shouldn't of done it" or "I must've been crazy."

Cecile refused to talk to Johanna and kept her eyes averted. And Rebecca was getting sicker. Her cheeks were flushed and her forehead felt hot to the touch.

A weak sun did little to warm the travellers as they made their way along the desolate road. Rebecca eventually fell asleep on a blanket, her blond hair spread about her face, her thumb in her mouth. Johanna started to relax. She fell asleep to the steady rhythm of the horse's hooves.

A sudden shout and the horse's startled neigh woke her up.

"Stop right 'ere!" Two men had rushed out of the bushes, grabbed the reins, and were forcing the wagon to stop.

"What're you doing?" demanded Daniel. He tugged on the reins, trying to wrestle them back from the men.

Johanna could feel Cecile trembling beside her. She crawled to where the baby had started wailing and picked her up.

"If you know what's good for you, let go of them reins!" answered the man who had spoken first. He was a large, burly man with a swollen face, crooked nose, and small eyes. He waved a long knife in the air as he spoke.

"You'd b-b-better listen," the other man said. His eyes moved up and down the road, and then darted back to the other man.

"Daniel! Stop!" Johanna said. She stroked Rebecca's sweating face and tried to comfort her, but the baby wouldn't stop crying. Daniel continued to struggle with the men. "The baby!" Johanna shouted.

"Damn!" Daniel stopped yanking on the reins and kept a wary eye on the man's knife.

"That's better," the big man said. He pulled the reins out of Daniel's hands and passed them over to the other man.

"Got them, Karl," his partner said, fumbling with the leather.

"What do you want?" said Daniel.

"Keep quiet!" Karl shouted. "Get down from the wagon."

"Do what he says," begged Johanna.

"Get down, I said!"

"All right," grumbled Daniel. He scrambled down and leaned against the wagon.

"That's better," Karl said. Without any warning, he punched Daniel in the face, pushed him to the ground, and kicked him in the ribs. Daniel groaned, blood seeping from his mouth and nose.

Cecile screamed. Johanna gasped and held the crying baby tightly to her chest.

Karl spat onto the road. He strode over to the girls and brandished his knife. "Hand over your money. An' be quick about it," he said to the girls.

"We don't have anything," said Johanna.

"We're only poor travellers," said Cecile.

Karl snorted. "We'll see about that!" He jumped onto the wagon and leaned over them. The smell of his unwashed body made Johanna retch.

"Get down," he ordered.

"But —" Johanna protested.

"You heard me. Down!"

Johanna's legs were shaking. Holding Rebecca, she stepped down from the wagon. Cecile followed close behind.

"That's better," Karl said. He leered at them. "Hey, Hans! Which one d'you want?"

"What?" Hans asked.

"These girls aren't bad looking. We could have some fun. One for you; one for me."

"You n-n-never said n-n-nothin' about that."

"Well, I hadn't thought about it neither, till I seen them." He licked his lips and stared at Johanna. "Do you like blonds or brunettes?"

"Let's g-g-get on with this, all right?" said Hans. "We d-d-don't want no t-t-trouble."

Daniel was groaning where he lay on the ground. Johanna shivered and the sweat ran down her spine. Rebecca was squirming in her arms; her diaper was wet, soaking through to Johanna's dress.

Karl looked up and down the road. He shrugged and said, "Guess we should." Pointing to the girls' belts, he said, "Throw your moneybags on the ground."

With shaking fingers, Cecile unfastened her bag and threw it down where Hans picked it up.

"You." Karl pointed to Cecile. "Back to the wagon."

"Cecile," Johanna said. "Take the baby."

Cecile nodded and took Rebecca from Johanna. She climbed back into the wagon and began to rock the crying baby.

"Now you," said Karl.

I can't do it, Johanna thought. *I need the money to save Rebecca.* She swallowed hard and shook her head.

"No?" Karl stalked over to her.

"No," Johanna said, her voice trembling.

"No one says 'no' to me!" Karl grabbed Johanna's arms and pinned them together. Her legs were shaking. Gritting her teeth, she kicked Karl in the shins as hard as she could.

"Hey!" He tightened his grip. "None of that!"

"Let me go!" Johanna yelled as she struggled to break free.

"Shut up!" Karl said. He struck Johanna hard on the face. Her cheek stung and her eyes watered. He hit her again and reached for her moneybag. She struggled to get away but he held her fast. He pushed Johanna down to the ground and pressed his hand on her mouth. She struggled to get up but he was as heavy as a fallen tree as he straddled her, trying to get her moneybag. She could scarcely breathe. What little air she inhaled was sour and sickening.

"The baby!" gasped Johanna. "The baby's sick."

Just then, Hans cried, "S-s-someone's coming!"

"Damn!" Karl yanked the moneybag from Johanna's belt, but the coins spilled onto the ground.

"C-c-come on, Karl!"

"All right," Karl said. "Let's go!"

The two men ran off into the fields and were soon hidden by the tall grass.

Johanna couldn't stop shaking. Cecile was weeping. Rebecca was howling. Daniel was crouched on the ground, dazed.

"Whoa!" A tall man on horseback looked down at the group in astonishment. "What is going on here?"

Johanna struggled to stand up, but she collapsed back onto the ground.

The man jumped off his horse. "Don't be afraid. I will help you." But Johanna didn't hear what he said. She had fainted.

———◆◆◆———

Johanna floated on a cinnamon-scented cloud. Brightly coloured birds flew about in the perfumed air. Nutmeg trees waved their branches on the ground far below. Johanna felt as if she were wrapped in a warm cocoon. She never wanted to leave.

"Johanna! Wake up!" Cecile was shaking her shoulder. Her voice sounded far away.

Johanna opened her eyes, blinked several times, and squeezed them shut. Her head was throbbing and her face ached. She opened her eyes again. She was lying on a blanket in the wagon. Someone had put her bag under her head for a pillow.

"Rebecca!" Johanna sat up with a start. Everything spun around. She felt sick to her stomach, leaned forward, and vomited over the side of the wagon.

"Don't worry," said Cecile. "She's fine."

"Lie still," said a man's voice.

"Do like he says," Daniel said.

Johanna groaned and lay back down on the blanket.

"Here. Drink this." Johanna looked up into a pair of warm brown eyes. The young man lifted her head and put a flask to her lips.

Johanna couldn't stop shaking. She sipped the brandy and choked. The liquid burned. "What happened?"

"You fainted," said Cecile.

"Out like a light," Daniel added.

"I'm sorry," Johanna said.

"There's nothing to be sorry about," said Cecile. "You were very brave!"

"I agree," said the man. He handed Johanna her moneybag. "I have taken the liberty of putting your coins back into your bag."

She looked at the man and blushed. "Thank you. But … who *are* you?"

The man laughed. "You fainted during my formal introduction." He bowed and said, "Benjamin Mendoza, at your service." A young man in his early twenties, he wore a white cravat tucked into a dark green waistcoat, brown jacket and breeches, white knee-stockings, and riding boots.

Another man stood by the side of the wagon. He held the reins of two horses. Mendoza followed Johanna's glance. "That is my servant. Clumsy Sam, we call him."

"Glad to make your acquaintance," said Sam. He bowed and his hat fell off.

"You can see why we call him that," said Mendoza, laughing. "But a better man you will not find in all the Netherlands." Sam retrieved his hat.

His large ears were turning a definite shade of red.

"Thank you for helping us, sir," said Cecile. "My name is Fraulein Hansen. This is Fraulein Richter —"

"Cecile," said Johanna, blushing. "I must correct you."

Cecile eyes opened wide in astonishment. "About what?"

Turning towards Mendoza, Johanna said, "My name is Johanna Eisen."

"I thought it was —" said Cecile.

"I can explain," Johanna said. But Cecile turned her stony face away. "Cecile," Johanna repeated. "I'm sorry."

"I don't wish to intrude, but the day is growing short," said Mendoza. "There is a good inn not far away, on the outskirts of Bremen. If you will allow me, I will accompany you there."

"Thank you," said Johanna.

Cecile nodded.

"I guess it won't do no harm," said Daniel, taking the reins in his hands and clicking his tongue. "My head feels like it's gonna roll off of my shoulders, my chest feels like the horse stepped on it, and my throat's dry as a desert."

Chapter Eleven

At the Inn

When they reached the inn, Mendoza rode up to the wagon, tipped his hat, and said, "I must leave you now. The fair is tomorrow and I have wares to sell."

"You're a merchant?" Johanna asked. Mendoza nodded.

"Mendoza and Sons, Spice Merchants." He grinned. "The name of the business was wishful thinking on my father's part. He hoped for many sons, but alas, I am the only one."

"Spice merchants?" Johanna felt stupid asking such an obvious question, but longed to hear the sound of this man's voice again.

"Our motto is, 'Spices from the Four Corners of the Earth.'" Mendoza bowed again.

"That's why I smelled spices when I fainted." Johanna blushed. "When you carried me to the wagon …"

Mendoza smiled. "It would seem that I can never get the smell of spices out of my clothes."

"I like the smell of spices," Johanna said, blushing even more.

"Even pepper?"

"Even pepper."

Mendoza chuckled.

"Thank you for everything, sir," said Cecile.

"Thank you, indeed," said Johanna.

"I was glad to be of service." Mendoza smiled at them once more, then guided his horse away from the wagon. Johanna watched as Clumsy Sam followed his master down the road. Her throat tightened as she watched Mendoza leave.

"You want *what*?" The woman stood at the door of the inn and blocked their way. Her blue eyes were small and alert, like a bird searching for worms. Wisps of greying hair escaped from her lace cap. She wiped her round face with a soggy handkerchief.

"We need a room for the night," Johanna said.

"Tonight? You must be joking!" the woman said. "With the fair starting tomorrow and people coming to town from everywhere?" She stood facing them, her hands on her hips. "Impossible." She began to shut the door.

"Wait!" Johanna said. "I have a baby with me!"

"A baby?" The woman opened the door. "What baby?"

Johanna lifted her cloak, but the baby began to cry when the cold air hit her face. The woman reached over and touched Rebecca's head. "I always did have a soft heart for a baby," she said. "I have one small room left. I was saving it for a gentleman, but he hasn't shown up yet. Likely won't come before tomorrow, it being so late now. Come in. My name is Frau Hesse. I own this inn."

Johanna had never felt so dirty and exhausted in her life. Her cheek was throbbing and she badly needed to go to the bathroom.

"Do you want the room?" asked Frau Hesse.

"How much will it be?" Johanna asked.

"Five schillings."

"We'll take it," Johanna said. "Thank you."

Frau Hesse pointed a finger at Daniel. "You can sleep in the stable, near the horses. It's warm and dry."

Daniel nodded. "I'll be fine sleepin' with the horses. Won't be the first time; won't be the last."

"Please wait a moment," said Cecile. "I need to talk to Johanna alone."

"All right," said Frau Hesse, shrugging. "Don't take too long about it. There's lots of travellers who'll be glad to have that room." She straightened her cap. "I'll be right back."

"What's the matter?" whispered Johanna after Frau Hesse had gone.

Cecile sighed. "I don't want to talk to you or have anything to do with you, but I don't have a choice." She lowered her voice. "Those robbers … took all my money. Will you help me?"

Johanna's heart sank. She doubted she now had enough money to last the journey. *I must have faith.* "Don't worry. I'll pay for tonight's lodgings."

"Thank you."

"Have you decided then?" asked Frau Hesse, hurrying back. Johanna nodded. "Right. Come with me. And you," she said, pointing to Daniel, "take your sorry horse to the stable."

As he led his horse away, Daniel muttered, "Women! They like to order a man around. Make our lives a misery." He looked back at Frau Hesse with a mixture of admiration and resentment.

The girls followed Frau Hesse through the main room and up a set of narrow stairs.

"I own and run this inn," she said, "leastways since my poor husband passed away five years ago. From the gout, it was. How the man suffered, I can't begin to tell you!

"All his joints hurt something awful. His big toes were always throbbing. Many a day he'd have to stay in bed, so bad was the pain. He was a good man, God rest his soul." She stopped at the top of the stairs and wiped her face. "Ah well, life brings good and bad to us all. We have to make the best of it, that's what I always say."

Frau Hesse unlocked the door and stood aside as they walked in. "Here we are."

The spotless wooden floor gleamed in the light from the candle Frau Hesse was holding. A white pitcher and basin stood on a washstand. A bed with clean linens was set against one wall. A fresh breeze from the river blew in through the open window.

"The girl will bring you water to wash up," said Frau Hesse. "Come down when you're ready for supper." She gazed at Rebecca, who was thrashing about in Johanna's arms. She sighed. "I had six babies. Five died. God rest their precious souls. Only the boy's left now." She smoothed the quilt on the bed. "I must go now. Lots to do. Never a minute's rest." She hurried out of the room and shut the door behind her.

Johanna put Rebecca on the bed, took off her cloak, and walked over to Cecile. Putting her hand on Cecile's shoulder, she said, "Thank you for saying I was brave back there."

Cecile refused to answer and only shook off Johanna's hand.

"What's wrong?" asked Johanna.

"Why did you lie to me again?"

"I had to change my name," said Johanna. "I thought Frau Taubman wouldn't give me a job if she knew I was Jewish. So, I had to pretend —"

"And you had to lie to me, too?" Cecile sniffed. "I was your friend."

Johanna looked down at the floor. "I didn't know if I could trust you."

"Obviously."

"I wanted to," said Johanna, "but I wasn't sure."

"And can you trust me now?"

Johanna hesitated. "I hope so."

"At least that's an honest answer." Cecile sat down on the bed and patted Rebecca's back. "So, is Eisen your real name? Or is that another lie?"

"It's my real name. I swear!" Johanna paused. "Cecile? Can't we be friends again?"

"I don't know," said Cecile, shaking her head. "Just ... please don't talk to me for a while. I need to think." She lay down on the bed and turned her back to Johanna.

As if sensing the anger between the two girls, Rebecca started to cry. Johanna picked her up and tried to distract her by showing her a tree outside the window, gulls flying in the darkening sky, and the long barges on the river. Finally Rebecca stopped crying, with only an occasional hiccup.

Just then, a servant brought in a kettle with warm water. Johanna washed the baby and changed her diaper. She rinsed the soiled diapers and hung them to dry on some hooks on the wall.

———◆◆◆———

The main room was filled with people who were staying at the inn. It looked inviting, as candles flickered on the walls and a fire crackled in the fireplace. When Johanna and Cecile entered the room, Frau Hesse persuaded some people to make room for them at a table near the fire.

"I made this myself," said Frau Hesse, ladling turnip stew into wooden bowls. Johanna held

Rebecca in her lap, mashed the stew with her spoon, blew on it, and fed the baby. She gulped her food down with loud slurping noises.

"Rebecca is just like my brother," Cecile said, her chin in her hand. "He never takes time to chew, either."

Johanna let out her breath. At last, Cecile was talking to her. "My little brother and sister were like that, too."

"If you don't mind, I'll sit with you for a minute," Frau Hesse said. "I need a bit of a break and it's nice to visit with two young women, instead of the rowdy bunch I usually get." She sat down hard on the bench beside Cecile. "So, what brings you to Bremen? It's unusual to see young women travelling alone."

"We —" Johanna began.

"I have a brother here," said Cecile. "I'm supposed to meet him."

"Really?" said Frau Hesse, raising her eyebrows. "Where does he live?"

"Just a minute. I've got the address somewhere." Cecile searched in her bag. "Here." She held the paper out to Frau Hesse.

"Can't read," said Frau Hesse, shrugging. "What does it say?"

"Johanna can read." Cecile handed the paper to Johanna.

"It says Antoine — that's her brother — lives at Kolpingstrasse, Number 17."

"Kolpingstrasse?"

"Do you know where that is?" asked Cecile.

Frau Hesse nodded. "I know Bremen like the back of my hand. That street is just a few blocks from the market square. The Rathaus — that's the town hall — is there. Nice building, all carved with arches and statues. And St. Peter's Cathedral. It's over five hundred years old." She lowered her voice. "They say there's a cellar under the cathedral, filled with dried-up corpses." Her voice returned to normal. "And then there's the new Schütting, the merchants' hall. We have a nice town here."

"So it seems!" Johanna said. *Will I ever have a home again?* she wondered.

"How can I send a message to my brother?" said Cecile. "I hope … I hope he's all right."

Johanna touched Cecile lightly on the arm. "I hope he is, too." Cecile looked at Johanna with surprise, but didn't move her arm away.

"Wait a minute." Frau Hesse stood up, walked towards the kitchen, opened the door and called, "Peter! Come here!" A young boy of about ten years old followed her back to their table. His hair was bright red and freckles were sprinkled all over his face.

"This is my son, Peter," Frau Hesse said. "This young lady needs a message taken to her brother. To the old part of town."

"I can take it." Peter grinned. "Mama, can I ride the horse into town?"

Frau Hesse wagged a finger at Peter. "You'll go in the morning. I'll not have you riding in the dark."

"Yes, Mama!" Peter said, hugging his mother.

"Off, boy! You're getting me all wet!" Peter moved away but kept grinning at his mother.

"Frau Hesse," said Johanna. "May I send a message, too?" She was patting Rebecca's back to help her burp.

"Why not?" Frau Hesse said. "Where to?"

Johanna swallowed hard. "Is there a good doctor in Bremen?"

Frau Hesse looked at Johanna sharply. "What's wrong? Are you sick?"

"No. I'm just … I'm worried about my baby."

"She's a nice baby," said Peter, putting his finger out for Rebecca to clasp.

"What's wrong with her?" asked Frau Hesse.

"She's got a bit of a rash," said Johanna. "That's all." Just then, Rebecca gave a loud belch and grinned, proud of what she'd done.

"Here, let me see." Frau Hesse held out her arms to the baby. Johanna handed Rebecca to her. Frau Hesse lifted the baby's dress and looked under her diaper. She examined the baby's arms and legs, and gently stroked her head.

An awful thought crept into Johanna's mind as she watched Frau Hesse with the baby.

What if … what if I left Rebecca here with Frau Hesse? She seems like a good woman. She would take care of her. She would feed and clothe her. She would be kind to her. Then I'd be free to continue the journey alone. I could go to Amsterdam, get a job, and send for Mama. She tried to brush the thought away, but she felt like an insect caught in the sticky strands of a spider's web.

No! I can't abandon Rebecca — now or ever. She took a big breath and clenched her fists. *I must do the right thing. That is what freedom means. To make the right choice.*

"She doesn't look very sick to me," said Frau Hesse, smiling at the baby and handing her back to Johanna. "But if you want a good doctor, Doctor Weiss is best for sick children.

"Why, I remember when Peter was a baby. Such a bad case of the croup he had. Couldn't stop coughing for a day and a night. We were afraid he wouldn't survive. But the doctor fixed him up real good. And look at him now." She stopped to take a breath and put an arm around her son. "Peter, you know where Doctor Weiss lives, don't you?"

"Yes, Mama."

"Good. You'll take a message to the doctor, too."

"I'll write it as soon as I put the baby to sleep," Johanna said. She held Rebecca in her arms and rocked her gently. She hummed Mama's lullaby.

> *Sleep, little baby, safely sleep.*
> *The birds are singing in the woods.*
> *They sing and hop in the grass so green.*
> *They'll bring the baby something good.*

Rebecca's eyes started to close as she cuddled into the warmth of Johanna's body. Johanna felt comforted by the trust Rebecca had in her.

"Good. It's settled," said Frau Hesse. "Now boy, back to work." She pinched Peter on the cheek.

"Mama! I'm too old for that!"

"You'll never be too old for me to pinch your cheek!"

"Yes I am, Mama!" Peter walked back to the kitchen, from where Johanna soon heard a loud clattering of pots and pans.

"Now then," said Frau Hesse. "Is there anything else you'll be needing?"

"No," said Johanna. "Thank you for your help."

"Yes, thank you," said Cecile.

Frau Hesse stood up quickly. "I must go. Lots to do. Never a minute's rest." She hurried away, her flesh jiggling with every step she took.

Chapter Twelve

The Reunion

That night, Johanna walked with Rebecca until the sick baby fell asleep at last. Johanna laid her gently on the bed and covered her with the quilt.

"Sleep well, little one," she said, kissing her on the forehead. By the light of the candle, Johanna wrote their messages. Cecile carried them down to Peter.

Johanna rinsed out the dirty diaper and hung it to dry along with the others. She smiled to see them hanging like a line of tired soldiers in a row. Every part of her body felt heavy as she put on her nightgown and climbed into bed.

"Cecile?"

"What?"

"Please don't kick me tonight."

"What are you talking about?" Cecile said. "I never kick in my sleep."

"Right," said Johanna, sighing.

Although the room was cold, Johanna quickly warmed up under the thick down quilt and fell asleep. Rebecca slept through the night. Everyone was feeling more cheerful the next morning.

On the way downstairs, they met Frau Hesse coming upstairs with a pile of linens. "Peter went out early this morning," she said. "Couldn't wait to saddle the horse! Hurry down, breakfast is ready."

Daniel was finishing his coffee as they came into the room. "It's about time you woke up," he said.

Cecile buttered the rye bread while Johanna spooned some oatmeal into a bowl, poured milk on top, and blew on it until it had cooled. She held Rebecca on her lap and fed the squirming baby while she tried to eat, too.

Daniel cleared his throat. "Well ... I'll be leaving today." He blew into his handkerchief. The sound was like honking geese. "I gotta get home."

Johanna nodded.

"So, when you're finished eating, pack your bags and I'll take you to the station."

"I won't be going," said Johanna. "I have to wait for the doctor."

"And I have to wait for my brother," said Cecile.

Daniel shrugged. "Do what you want. I'm going to see to the horse."

Johanna began to play a game with Rebecca. She hid the spoon under the table and brought it out again. Each time, Rebecca laughed and tried to grab it from Johanna.

"Cecile, have you noticed that Rebecca has changed?" Johanna said.

"How?"

"It's as if she's suddenly older."

"What do you mean?"

"It's like … she's waking up. You know … like when you're sleeping and the sun shines on your face and wakes you up."

"You're right," said Cecile. "She's looking around all the time and noticing more and —"

"Paying attention to everything. Not like at the orphanage, where all the babies stopped crying after a while. As if they knew we couldn't talk to them or pay attention to them. And then they gave up trying." Johanna shuddered. "I'm glad we left that horrible place."

"So am I. And you know —"

"Quiet," Johanna whispered. A tall, slender man had entered the inn. He glanced around the room, as if searching for someone.

"What is it?"

"Someone just walked in," she said. "He looks important. Maybe he's from the duke." She swallowed hard. "Maybe they're still trying to find us."

"What should we do?" Cecile asked in a shaking voice. Her back was to the stranger.

"Nothing," Johanna said. "Don't turn around. Maybe he won't see us." She tried to look at the stranger without catching his attention. He wore a dark brown, fitted buttoned coat, a white cravat tucked into his silk waistcoat, knee-length breeches, white knee stockings, and high-heeled leather shoes with shiny buckles.

Rebecca began to cry and the man looked in their direction. He gave a start when he saw Cecile. He strode over to their table.

"Cecile!" cried the man. A smile lit up his face. "Is it really you?"

"Antoine!" Cecile stood up and almost knocked over the bench. "God be praised!"

Antoine took Cecile in his arms and hugged her tightly. Then, holding her at arm's length, he said, "How glad I am to see you! I was worried you didn't get my message." Antoine swallowed hard. "Or that you might have caught the plague."

"I'm fine," said Cecile. She was laughing and crying at the same time. She held onto Antoine's arm as if she would never let go. "But, tell me, what happened to Mama and Papa."

Antoine pressed his lips together. "They passed away quickly," he said. "At least that was a blessing."

Cecile shuddered and put her head on Antoine's chest.

"We must go on with our lives," Antoine said. "It is what they would have wished."

Cecile nodded, wiped her eyes, and blew her nose.

"Let's sit down," Antoine said. "How long have you been here? Why did you leave the orphanage? Why didn't you answer my letters?"

"One question at a time!" Cecile said. "First, you must meet … my friend … Johanna Richter — I mean, Eisen. She helped me come here."

"Eisen?" Antoine raised his eyebrows. "Are you a Jew?"

"Yes," Johanna said, straightening her back. She wouldn't lie again about who she was. "I am."

Antoine narrowed his eyes and then grabbed Cecile by the arm. "Come, Cecile. We must go."

Johanna could feel the tears welling up in her eyes.

Cecile shook Antoine's hand off and said, "Stop! Johanna saved my life!"

"What are you talking about?"

"We were attacked by robbers on the road. Johanna fought them off. They took my money, but might have done much worse if it hadn't been for Johanna."

"I see," said Antoine, biting his lower lip. Johanna heard the clatter of pots and pans from the kitchen, the low voices of the other customers, and the crackling of the fire.

Antoine took off his hat and bowed his head. "I owe you an apology," he said in a tight voice. "I am very grateful to you for helping my sister."

"I'm glad I could help," said Johanna, blushing.

Frau Hesse approached their table. She looked approvingly at Antoine. "Will you be wanting breakfast, sir?"

"No, thank you. Just coffee."

"Right away, sir."

Antoine sat down next to Cecile and crossed his arms on his chest. "Will you answer my questions now?"

"Of course," said Cecile. She grinned. "What were they again?"

"Why did you leave the orphanage? I thought you liked the job."

"I did at first."

"We both did," Johanna said. "But things changed."

"How?" They stopped talking while Frau Hesse poured coffee for Antoine. She soon bustled away.

"Did Cecile tell you we weren't allowed to talk to the babies or hold them?"

Antoine nodded. "I thought she must be exaggerating."

"I was not!" Cecile said. "We would have lost our jobs."

Antoine sipped his coffee and looking intently at the girls.

"The babies eventually stopped crying," Johanna said. "All they did was lie in their beds. But the worst thing was —"

"They started to die," Cecile said.

"They were sick?" Antoine asked.

Cecile shook her head. "It was more like —"

"A sickness of spirit," said Johanna. "As if they no longer wished to live."

"Is that when you decided to leave?" asked Antoine.

"Yes," Johanna said. "And to take this baby with me."

"And I decided to go with her," said Cecile, thrusting out her chin.

Antoine put his arm around Cecile. "I see that my little sister has grown up."

"You're not angry I ran away?"

"Of course not. It was an intolerable situation. But now," he said, gulping the last of his coffee, "we must go. The fair is today and I must attend to business." He smiled. "Not to mention bringing my sister home." He took a coin out of his bag and placed it on the table.

"Antoine?" said Cecile.

"Yes?"

"Johanna paid for our room last night. Could you…?"

"No," said Johanna, shaking her head.

"We must repay you," said Cecile. "You were kind to me and helped me."

"I'm sorry that I didn't trust you with my secret," Johanna said.

"I'm sorry I was unfair," said Cecile.

"Friends?"

"Friends."

"We really must go," said Antoine, standing up. He reached into his bag again and held out a few coins. "Please take this money to help you on your journey." He paused. "It is the least I can do."

Johanna nodded. "Thank you."

"Will you be all right?" asked Cecile.

"Yes," said Johanna. *I hope so.* "Don't worry about me."

Cecile hesitated, and then hugged Johanna. Because Rebecca was crushed between them, she began to cry. Both girls laughed. Wiping the tears from her eyes, Cecile went upstairs to get her things. When she came back, she was wearing her cloak and carrying her bag. Johanna accompanied them to the door and watched as they climbed into the waiting carriage.

Johanna called, "God be with you!"

Cecile hesitated for a moment. Then she called back, "God keep you safe!"

Taking Rebecca's hand, Johanna said, "Say 'bye bye.'" She waved the baby's hand as the carriage drove away.

The road was clogged with people on the way to the fair. They were walking, pulling carts, driving wagons and carriages, but Johanna didn't see them. They were talking and shouting, but Johanna didn't hear them. A gentle breeze rustled through the new leaves on the trees, but Johanna didn't feel it. She sat down on a bench by the door, took out her handkerchief, and wept.

Chapter Thirteen

The Kindness of Strangers

"Fraulein Eisen?"

"Mr. Mendoza!" Johanna stood up quickly. She wiped her eyes and blew her nose. She was sure she must look like a ragged street urchin.

"Are you all right?" Mendoza asked.

Johanna nodded. "Cecile left a moment ago."

"Where did she go?"

"Not far. To stay with her brother."

"But that is good, is it not?" He pointed to the bench. "May I?"

Johanna nodded. "It is. For her," she said, sniffling. "But I shall miss her."

"Of course you will." He paused. "But I'm glad you are still here."

"You are?"

"I couldn't stop thinking about you — a young woman, travelling alone with a child." He turned towards her and leaned closer. "Such a journey is not safe. I want to help you."

"You do?"

Rebecca was making gurgling noises and tried to grab Mendoza's cloak. He smiled at the baby and patted her head.

"I know a woman, a friend of my mother's, who has come to trade at the fair. She's almost finished her business and will return to Amsterdam by ship. I talked to her about you. She has agreed to have you accompany her."

"I'm very grateful, but I don't understand why you're helping me."

Rebecca was wiggling about and Johanna had trouble holding her and concentrating on the conversation at the same time.

"I will introduce you to the woman tomorrow morning. About eight, shall we say? Then you can decide." He smiled. "With a little luck, you should reach the city before the Sabbath."

Johanna's heart began to beat quickly. "The Sabbath? You ... know about the Sabbath?" She hesitated. "Are you ... are you Jewish, too?"

Mendoza nodded. "Of course I am. Couldn't you tell?" He placed a gentle hand on Johanna's arm. "I want to help a fellow Jew — especially a woman who is travelling alone." He gazed into her eyes. "I would feel more at ease if I knew you were safe."

Johanna released her breath. She hadn't realized she had been holding it. "Thank you. I accept your kind offer."

"It's settled then!" Mendoza said, standing up. "But now I must go."

"Wait! I've never been on a ship before!"

"Don't worry. You'll be fine. I've done the crossing many times. With all the fighting on land that is going on between the Netherlands and France, it is the safest and fastest way to get to Amsterdam."

"Thank you, Mr. Mendoza, with all my heart."

"You are most welcome." Mendoza tipped his hat. "Until tomorrow then." He walked briskly away from the inn.

"You see, Rebecca," Johanna said, hugging the baby. "God has brought us help." The baby gurgled and began to play with the buttons on Johanna's dress.

Daniel came by a few moments later. "Well, the horse is doing fine. Are you still waiting for the doctor?"

Johanna nodded. "I am. But I have good news. Mr. Mendoza has arranged a way for me to get to Amsterdam." She recounted their conversation.

"You're going with a total stranger?"

Johanna smiled. "You were a stranger once." Rebecca was squirming about on Johanna's lap.

Daniel scratched his head. "That's true."

"Anyway, I'll be travelling with a friend of his mother's."

"Hope you know what you're doing." Daniel took a large, grey handkerchief from his pocket and blew his nose. "See what you done? I'm using a handkerchief now, like you told me, instead of my sleeve."

"I'm glad to see it, Daniel."

"Right." He crumpled up the handkerchief and put it back in his pocket. "I have to get back to Hamburg."

"Daniel?"

"What?"

"Thank you for everything."

"You're welcome." He gazed down at Rebecca. "Have a safe journey. You and the baby." Rebecca reached out for Daniel's arm.

"You too," said Johanna. "And Daniel?"

"Yes?"

Johanna reached into her moneybag and took out a few coins. "Here's the money I owe you."

Daniel pushed the money back into her hand. "No need."

"What do you mean?"

"Well, you were robbed and beaten. I feel kind of responsible." Daniel looked down. "I won't charge you the rest."

"You won't?"

Daniel shook his head. "Take care of the baby. That's the main thing."

Johanna felt a lump in her throat and could only nod her head. Daniel tipped his cap, took one glance back, and hurriedly walked away.

Doctor Weiss had finished examining Rebecca.

"Nothing to worry about," the doctor said. He was a fat, balding man whose waistcoat buttons strained like a prisoner at his handcuffs.

"Are you sure?"

Doctor Weiss peered over his spectacles at Johanna. "Young lady, there is nothing to worry about. This baby has a rash. That is all. Common in babies. Probably an imbalance of the humours."

"What should I do?"

"Well, let me see," he said, stroking his chin. "I could bleed her, or purge her ..."

"No!"

The doctor looked up sharply. "Very well, then. Perhaps that won't be necessary. Keep her warm and give her plenty to drink. She should be fine in a few days."

"Thank you, doctor."

"And you? That is quite a bruise on your face."

"Oh, it's nothing," said Johanna, touching her sore cheek.

"A cold compress will help." He paused. "That will be three schillings."

Johanna handed over the money. She spent the rest of the day working on her lace, taking care of Rebecca, and worrying about money.

— Chapter Fourteen —

On the Road to Emden

"Good morning, Fraulein Eisen!" Mendoza said, as he entered the inn. "Mrs. de Pina is waiting outside in the carriage. Are you ready?"

"Yes, I am," said Johanna, standing up and smoothing her dress.

As she struggled with her bag and the baby, Mendoza said, "Sam will help you."

"Thank you," said Johanna, handing her bag to Sam.

"We must go. Mrs. de Pina doesn't like to be kept waiting."

Johanna paid for her room and said goodbye to Frau Hesse. She hurried out of the inn.

Sam tripped three times and dropped the bag once on their way out. *I'm glad I gave Sam my bag, and not the baby.* Mendoza helped Johanna into the carriage and Sam placed her bag at her feet.

The woman seated across from Johanna wore a dark woollen dress covered with a fur-trimmed travelling cloak. Her hair was streaked with grey, her eyes were dark brown, and her nose was long and straight. Her mouth was turned down in a disapproving frown.

"Mrs. de Pina," Mendoza began, "allow me to introduce you to —"

Mrs. de Pina raised her eyebrows. "So, this is the young woman you told me about."

"Fraulein Johanna Eisen."

"I understand you wish to travel with me to Amsterdam?" Mrs. de Pina said.

"Yes, ma'am." Johanna felt like a fish being inspected at the market. Rebecca kept wriggling about and tried to reach the swaying feather in Mrs. de Pina's hat.

"Why do you wish to go to Amsterdam, Fraulein Eisen?"

"To start a new life for myself and my ... baby sister."

"A new life?"

"My parents died of the plague. And I heard there were jobs in Amsterdam for lace workers." *I hate lying*, Johanna thought.

"Mendoza tells me you are Jewish."

Johanna nodded.

Mrs. de Pina sniffed. "I am not acquainted with your family. I don't know you."

"I don't know you, either," Johanna said.

"You have spirit, fraulein."

"My mother used to say that, too." The thought of Mama almost made Johanna cry.

"Very well," Mrs. de Pina said. She smiled a whisper of a smile. "This should be an interesting voyage."

Mendoza tipped his hat. "I must go. I wish you a safe journey."

"Be off then," said Mrs. de Pina, waving him away. "But do take care. These are dangerous times."

"Thank you again for your help, Mr. Mendoza," said Johanna.

"You are most welcome," said Mendoza. "Perhaps we shall see each other in Amsterdam?"

"I hope so," said Johanna, blushing.

With these words, Mendoza closed the carriage door and shouted, "Driver, you may leave now!"

"Yes, sir!" the driver answered. He flicked the reins and the carriage began to move away from the inn.

"Benjamin Mendoza," Mrs. de Pina said, "is a fine young man."

Johanna nodded. She didn't want to show Mrs. de Pina how much she hoped to see him again. She busied herself with straightening Rebecca's clothes and settling her on her lap.

"Perhaps it will prove more interesting to talk with a woman for a change." Mrs. de Pina cleared her throat. "The only thing men want to talk about is business. Do you not agree, Fraulein Eisen?"

"Yes ma'am. And politics."

"Mind you, business is important. A person must make a living." Mrs. de Pina sighed. "After my husband died ten years ago, I took over his business." Rebecca was starting to fall asleep and she felt heavy in Johanna's arms.

"What kind of business is it?" asked Johanna. "I hope I'm not prying."

"You are not." Mrs. de Pina squared her shoulders. "I buy and sell goods." She paused. "I enjoy going to fairs, but lately it has become more and more dangerous to travel."

Johanna shuddered. "I know what you mean. We were attacked on the road by robbers."

"Terrible! You were lucky to come away unscathed."

Johanna touched her cheek. "Mr. Mendoza saved us."

Mrs. de Pina gazed at Johanna. "You were fortunate. Do you object to a woman in business?"

"I've never thought about it, one way or the other." Johanna swallowed hard. "Mama worked after Papa died and I have worked, too."

"Where do you come from, fraulein?"

"Hamburg." Johanna felt uncomfortable under Mrs. de Pina's scrutiny. She knew her clothes were wrinkled and dirty; she hadn't washed properly for days; she probably smelled like a sewer.

"I know what it is to be poor," said Mrs. de Pina, as if reading Johanna's mind.

"You do?"

Mrs. de Pina nodded. "I come from a poor family. It was my good fortune to meet my husband, who made a good living. I worked with him while he was alive and learned the business well." She pressed her lips together. "I decided a long time ago that I would never be poor or depend on my children in my old age." Mrs. de Pina looked sharply at Johanna. "You said you make lace?"

"Yes, ma'am," said Johanna. *I don't want to tell her about the orphanage. Not yet.*

Mrs. de Pina nodded. "Honest work."

"I think it's lovely that you have a business of your own."

"My older children help me."

"How many do you have?"

"I gave birth to ten. Six survived."

Johanna gasped. Caring for only one baby was more work than she had ever expected.

Mrs. de Pina smiled. "Most of them are grown and married. However, I still have two at home, and that is a blessing."

Johanna nodded. She could feel every lurch and bump as the carriage continued on its way. The bruise on her cheek was only one of the aches and pains she felt. She tried her best to hold Rebecca against her body; to shield the baby from the swaying and rocking of the carriage.

After an hour's travel, grey clouds gathered in a darkening sky. The wind began to lash the leaves in the trees. They were still far from Oldenburg when the first large drops of rain began to fall. The drops turned into torrents pelting the carriage without mercy. The wind rocked the carriage madly about.

They passed other struggling carriages on the road. Each time, they were forced to the side where the mud was thickest. Each time, Johanna prayed their carriage wouldn't overturn.

Why did I undertake this dangerous journey? I want to be home again. I don't want to be a grownup; to be responsible for another human being. She looked down at the baby. Her resolve strengthened. *This is reason enough — to save this child from almost certain death.*

The driver urged the struggling horses through the thick mud. Several times, the carriage got stuck. Only with great effort was he able to free its wheels so they could continue on their way.

Johanna felt sick to her stomach. Mrs. de Pina's face looked pale in the dim light. Rebecca wailed with every clap of thunder and bolt of lightning. It took three endless hours to reach Oldenburg.

The driver finally stopped the carriage at an inn. He jumped down from his seat, opened the door, and shouted, "We'd better stop here till the storm lets up!" His hat and coat were soaked through.

"I agree," said Mrs. de Pina. "We must stop or I feel my bones will break."

They got down from the carriage and entered the smoky inn. After they had taken off their wet cloaks, they ordered a meal of bread, cheese, and fried onions. While they waited, they tried to warm themselves near the fire.

Johanna shivered. She felt as though she would never be warm or dry again. She fed Rebecca bread and warm milk, and finally the baby fell asleep.

After an hour, the rain stopped. "My mother used to say if the sky has enough blue in it to make a pocket handkerchief, then the rest of the day will be clear."

"Let us hope she was right," said Mrs. de Pina.

The driver wanted to stay in Oldenburg for the night, but Mrs. de Pina gave him an extra coin to continue on the road to Emden. He reluctantly agreed to take them, all the while uttering dire warnings.

They climbed back into the carriage. The road was muddy, but the spring sun and a brisk wind soon dried it up.

It took them the rest of the long day to reach Emden. It was already dark when the driver stopped at a small inn. Mrs. de Pina had booked a room there when she'd passed through on her way to the fair.

"At last," Mrs. De Pina said, getting down stiffly from the carriage. "I cannot stand the jostling of this carriage for one more minute! Tomorrow, we shall book passage on a ship to take us across the sea to Amsterdam. With luck, we shall arrive there before the Sabbath."

Johanna was grateful to get out of the carriage; to walk again on firm ground. Her damp clothes clung to her body, her hair was a tangled mess, and she desperately needed to go to the bathroom.

"The crossing is bearable," said Mrs. de Pina. "But one must try not move from the time one leaves Emden until one arrives in Amsterdam."

Johanna was too tired to care.

Chapter Fifteen

The Sea Passage

All kinds of sailing ships and fishing boats were anchored in the busy harbour. The piers were cluttered with wooden barrels, huge crates, and thick ropes coiled in neat circles. Sailors with heavy loads on their backs walked up and down gangways leading to the ships. Merchants haggled with each other as they stood on the wooden sidewalk. Passengers milled about, their trunks and bags at their feet.

Rebecca squirmed in Johanna's arms as she looked at the sky. A gull swooped onto the water and caught a fish in its beak. Rebecca raised her arm as she watched the bird fly away.

"Come," said Mrs. de Pina. "We must buy our tickets."

What if someone tries to stop me? We're still in Germany. What if I'm on a list of people the agent is supposed to look for? She straightened her back and tried not to look as nervous as she felt. She paid for her ticket, her hands trembling and her legs shaking. She let out her breath when the transaction was finally done.

"Which ship is ours?" Johanna asked.

"The *Prince William*," said Mrs. de Pina, pointing to a small, three-masted ship. "That kind of ship is known as a *fluyt*. It is named after William of Orange."

"It's beautiful," said Johanna. The ship was intricately decorated with carvings on its sides and stern. The two front sails were square; the sail near the stern was triangular.

"Welcome, ladies!" a voice boomed from the ship. A stocky man walked down the gangway. "I'm the first mate here. Name is Jon Visser. Can I see your tickets?"

After glancing at them, Visser nodded and handed the tickets back. "Follow me," he said as he picked up their bags. "Your quarters are below deck, on the port side."

"Port side?" asked Johanna.

"The left side, as you look forwards. Come along now. You're our only passengers and we must go."

As soon as they were on board, the gangway was pulled up. Visser called, "Prepare the sail!" The men released the ropes tying the sails down. They filled with air and billowed in the wind.

Johanna struggled to keep a firm grip on the baby while she held onto a rope beside some narrow steps, which were almost like a ladder, leading down into the ship.

"Here we are," said Visser, ducking under a doorway. They entered a small, immaculate room. Two beds were set into opposite walls; a small table was bolted to the floor; a lantern hung by a chain from a highly polished wooden ceiling.

"Make yourselves comfortable," Visser said. "We'll be on our way soon."

"How long does the crossing take?" Johanna asked.

"About two days."

"Two days!" Johanna gazed at the water through the small porthole. It seemed wide and deep and endless to her.

"Of course," Visser said. "What did you think?"

Johanna didn't have an answer.

"Don't worry," he said. "The weather is clear. We should reach Amsterdam by tomorrow afternoon."

"Thank you," said Mrs. de Pina. "We shall be fine."

"Have a good crossing then." Visser nodded and left the room. It seemed much bigger after he had gone.

Johanna sat on the narrow bed and held Rebecca on her lap. She named the things she touched — "table," "diaper," "cup." The baby followed her movements carefully and listened whenever she spoke.

Then Johanna pointed to herself and said, "Mama." The word came out of her mouth without thinking. But once out, it felt right.

"Mama," she repeated, hugging Rebecca to her chest.

"You are my child now," she whispered. "Not by birth, but because I saved your life. And because I love you."

The ship gave a sudden lurch. Johanna grabbed the table with one hand while she held onto Rebecca with the other. She heard the creak of the masts and felt the swaying of the ship as it sailed out of the harbour and into the open sea.

"Time to lie down," said Mrs. de Pina. She hung her hat on a hook and lay down on one of the beds.

"So early in the day?"

"Yes. Try not to move until we arrive, or you will be sick." Mrs. de Pina closed her eyes.

Johanna wanted to lie down, but Rebecca was looking at everything and squirmed in her arms.

The ship bucked and rolled and swayed as it made its way to the North Sea. It seemed to move in all four directions at once. The further the ship travelled, the worse Johanna felt. Her breakfast rose in her throat. She put Rebecca on the bed, and scarcely reached the bucket in time.

When there was nothing more to vomit, Johanna's chest kept heaving anyway. Her legs were shaking and her skin was clammy. Rebecca pointed to the bucket. Despite her nausea, Johanna said "bucket," laughing through her groans.

After an hour, Mrs. de Pina croaked, "Fraulein Eisen, I need you." Her face was pale and her hands trembled.

Johanna staggered over to Mrs. de Pina. "How can I help?"

"I cannot stand," Mrs. de Pina said. "Bring the bucket to me."

Her head spinning, Johanna hauled the bucket to Mrs. de Pina's bed. The older woman retched into it. When she was done, she lay back on her bed, gasping for air.

Johanna searched in her bag and found a glass bottle of water she had filled at the inn. She soaked a clean handkerchief in water and laid the cool cloth on Mrs. de Pina's head.

"Thank you, my dear," said Mrs. de Pina, as she closed her eyes.

Just then, the ship swayed to one side. Johanna lost her balance and was thrown to the other side of the room. Rebecca bumped her head on the wall. She howled and tears flowed down her cheeks.

Johanna tried to comfort her; tried not to retch and gag; tried not to vomit again. She sat on the bed, holding and rocking Rebecca until at last the baby quieted down. For the rest of the day, her attention was divided between helping Mrs. de Pina and seeing that the baby came to no further harm.

In the evening, someone knocked on the door. From her bed, Johanna called, "Who is it?"

A young boy entered the room. He carried a tray which he placed on the table. "I've brought a light supper for you, ladies." He wrinkled his nose. "Maybe I'd better take this bucket and bring you an empty one."

Johanna and Mrs. de Pina groaned.

Johanna raised herself from the bed and staggered out to the water closet in the hall. After she had relieved herself, she made her way back to the sour-smelling room. She was grateful that Rebecca was finally asleep. She lifted the cloth that covered the tray and poured a cup of steaming coffee.

She sipped the coffee, savouring the warmth of the liquid as it slid down her throat.

"Would you like a cup of coffee?" Johanna said.

Mrs. de Pina sat up and stretched. "I shall try," she said, as she grasped the cup with shaking fingers. She patted her dress, now dirty and wrinkled. "My dear, I wonder if I look as badly as I feel."

"No one can look as bad as I," said Johanna.

"Then we certainly are a pair!" said Mrs. de Pina. "I have taken this sea passage many times, but this is one of the worst."

"I didn't expect it to be such an ordeal."

"Ah well," said Mrs. de Pina. "One night and it will be over."

"That won't be soon enough for me!"

"Let us try to sleep now," said Mrs. de Pina. "The night will pass more quickly."

Johanna wondered if morning would ever come. From time to time, she tried giving Rebecca something to drink to keep her from disturbing Mrs. de Pina. Finally, when light began to seep in through the porthole, Johanna fell asleep.

She woke up to the sound of the ship's bell clanging to announce their arrival in Amsterdam.

She felt like a limp, smelly dishrag — all wrung out and badly needing a wash.

Mrs. de Pina stretched and rose unsteadily to her feet. "I shall arrange for the man to bring our bags."

Johanna picked up the baby and followed Mrs. de Pina up the narrow steps and down the gangway to the pier. She was grateful for the fresh air and the breeze playing around her skirts.

She followed Mrs. de Pina to a building marked ARRIVALS. They made their way to an office near the front door. A thin, stooped man was seated at a desk. His quill was busy scratching on some papers. He looked up from his work. "Yes?"

"We have just arrived on the *Prince William*," said Mrs. de Pina.

Johanna's heart was pounding. *What if this man turns me back? Where will I go? What will I do?* She tried to breathe slowly; to control the panic she was beginning to feel.

"I must examine your papers," said the man reaching his hand out. "Kindly show them to me."

Mrs. de Pina reached into her bag and handed her papers to the man. He scrutinized them. "Why did you leave the Netherlands?"

"I went to Germany on business," Mrs. de Pina said.

The man raised his eyebrows. "A woman alone?"

Mrs. de Pina drew herself erect. "Yes. And why not?"

"No reason, ma'am," said the man hastily. "Only it is rather unusual."

"Indeed," said Mrs. de Pina, a faint smile on her lips.

The man shuffled his papers. "What is your permanent address?"

"I reside in Amsterdam. Jodenbreestraat, number 136."

"These seem to be in order." The man stamped and signed the papers, before handing them back to Mrs. de Pina. "Your turn, young lady," he said, holding out his hand.

"Here, give me the baby," said Mrs. de Pina. Johanna handed Rebecca to her, loosened her bag, and found the papers. With trembling fingers, she handed them to the man.

He looked at Johanna. "You are a native of Hamburg?"

"Yes, sir."

"But, look here," the man said. "These are only travelling papers. You are not a citizen of Hamburg?"

"No, sir. I am Jewish. We are not allowed to become citizens." Johanna could feel her face getting red.

"I see." The man pursed his lips. "And why have you come to Amsterdam?"

"To work."

"You have a family here? A place to live?"

Johanna swallowed hard. "No, but —"

"But what?" The man crossed his arms and leaned back against his chair. "The law is very clear. You are not allowed to enter the Netherlands without a job or family. You will have to —"

Johanna's legs shook. *Will I be turned back when I am so close?*

"I have a job," she blurted out. She looked over at Mrs. de Pina and hoped the woman would understand. "I work for Mrs. de Pina."

The man raised his eyebrows. "Is that right?"

"Certainly. She is in my employ. She will work in my house."

Mrs. de Pina and Johanna shared a look of quiet understanding. Rebecca held out her arms and Johanna took the baby back. She snuggled against Johanna, sighed, and closed her eyes.

"I see." The man narrowed his eyes. "You will guarantee she will not become the responsibility of the state?"

"Yes, of course," said Mrs. de Pina.

"You must fill out a form," he said, riffling through the papers on his desk. "Now where did I put it?" At last, he pushed a paper towards them. "Here it is," he said. He pointed to the baby. "Whose baby is that?"

"She's mine," said Johanna, holding Rebecca tightly to her chest.

"And her papers? Where are they?"

"She … doesn't have any," said Johanna. "Our parents died, and I'm the only one she has left. Please …."

Mrs. de Pina said, "She will be my responsibility as well. Give me the papers. I will sign for the baby, too."

"Very well, then," said the man, as he searched for another form. Mrs. de Pina sat down at a table nearby and filled out both papers. When she had finished, the man looked them over, stamped and signed Johanna's papers, and handed them back to her. Johanna clutched them tightly in her hand.

The man smiled and said, "Welcome to the Netherlands."

"Thank you!" said Johanna, breathing a sigh of relief.

They hurried outside the office to an area where carriages were waiting for passengers. "Come quickly," said Mrs. de Pina. "It will be the Sabbath soon. We must get home before sunset."

Mrs. de Pina hired a carriage and they settled into their seats. "Driver, take us to Jodenbreestraat, number 136."

"Yes, ma'am!"

"And please hurry!"

Johanna breathed deeply until she felt her heart beating normally again. The baby had fallen asleep, her head on Johanna's arm. Her diaper was wet, but Johanna didn't want to disturb her. Besides, she felt so worn out, she could scarcely move.

"I do detest these border crossings," said Mrs. de Pina, smoothing out her dress and re-tying the ribbons under her hat.

"Mrs. de Pina, did you mean it?" Johanna said. "About my working for you?"

"Yes, why not? I see you are good with children and skilful with your hands." She paused. "I am grateful for your help during the crossing." She put her hand on Johanna's arm and smiled. "My dear, I am willing to try you out. That is, if you are willing to try *me* out!"

"Thank you. Thank you so much!"

"Then it is settled." Mrs. de Pina looked sharply at Johanna. "Rebecca isn't really your sister, is she?"

"No, but she is very precious to me."

"I can see that." Mrs. de Pina paused. "I believe it is time you told me the truth. Do you not agree?"

Chapter Sixteen

Haven

After Johanna had told her story, Mrs. de Pina peered at Johanna and sighed. "I see that you have had your share of troubles."

"You don't blame me for what I did?" Johanna said.

"Not at all," said Mrs. de Pina. "There is much of myself I see in you." She paused. "Enough said. You are in a new place, ready to begin a new life."

Mrs. de Pina opened the curtains of the carriage and pointed. "Now, you must look at Amsterdam!"

Johanna felt close to tears as she gazed out the window at the most beautiful city she had ever seen. Sunlight touched the slate roofs, making them glow in shades of gold and amber.

The streets were filled with carts, wagons, and horse-drawn carriages, all jostling for space. Women carried shopping baskets and hurried along the sidewalks. Men at street corners talked animatedly about what Johanna assumed were business matters. Children ran about, playing tag or rolling hoops or bouncing balls.

"Everyone seems so busy!" Johanna said. "How many people live here?"

"About 100,000. Among them are over four hundred Jewish families."

"So many! Where did they come from?"

"Most came from Spain and Portugal, after the Jews and the conversos were expelled over two hundred years ago. More recently, Jews have come from Germany, like you; others, from Poland."

"What are 'conversos'?" asked Johanna. Her heart beat with excitement as she tried to take in the sights of the city while listening to Mrs. de Pina.

"Jews who converted to Christianity, but still practised their religion in secret."

"In secret?"

"They had to hide all religious practices, like lighting candles for the Sabbath or eating matzo on Passover. All the important events — births, bar mitzvahs, weddings, deaths."

"I've never heard of them."

Mrs. de Pina smiled. "In fact you have already met one."

"I have?"

"That young man who helped you, Benjamin Mendoza, comes from a prosperous converso family." When she heard Mendoza's name, Johanna blushed. She hoped Mrs. de Pina didn't notice.

"They have done very well for themselves. In fact, many Jews are shareholders in the East India Company. Of course, the most important point is that, since 1657, Jews have been allowed to become citizens of this country."

"Citizens! Is it really true?"

"It certainly is." Mrs. de Pina sighed. "It is like a miracle to live in a country where we can be treated fairly, and even have rights as citizens."

The carriage made its way over several bridges and through the narrow, winding streets of the city. Everywhere Johanna looked, she saw patches of colourful flowers.

The carriage finally came to a stop. "Here we are. Home at last. And with an hour to spare before the Sabbath!"

They alighted from the carriage in front of a white, three-story house. Four steps led up to the main entrance. Other steps on either side of the door went down to a lower level. Johanna was amazed at how orderly and clean everything looked.

"Come along," said Mrs. de Pina, as she pushed open a heavy oak door that led into a large entrance hall.

A tall, thin woman hurried over to them. "Welcome home, madam," she said. "We were worried you wouldn't make it in time."

"I wasn't sure myself. Thank God, we have arrived safely." Beckoning to Johanna, Mrs. de Pina said, "I have brought someone with me. This is Fraulein Johanna Eisen, who accompanied me from Bremen with her baby, Rebecca."

"How do you do?" the woman said.

"Fraulein Eisen, this is Mrs. de Groot, our housekeeper. I don't know what I would do without her."

Johanna curtsied. "I'm very glad to meet you."

Mrs. de Groot took their hats and cloaks, and hung them on a coat tree in the entrance hall.

"Please arrange for our bags to be brought in. Then show Fraulein Eisen to a spare room," Mrs. de Pina said. "She will be our guest for the Sabbath, after which she will begin to work here. And Mrs. de Groot?"

"Yes, madam?"

"Johanna will need warm water and some clean clothes for the baby." Mrs. de Pina smiled. "I must have something that my children have outgrown."

"I shall see to everything right away," said Mrs. de Groot.

"Fraulein Eisen, we will call you when it is time to light the candles," said Mrs. de Pina. "Now please hurry."

"I will," said Johanna. "And thank you."

"Now, where are my children?!"

Mrs. de Groot left Johanna in a room on the third floor. It was plainly furnished with a four-poster bed covered with a quilt, an upholstered chair, and a small, inlaid writing table. The windows were hung with lace curtains and a worn Indian rug lay on the polished wooden floor.

Johanna put Rebecca on the bed and struggled to undress her. The baby was playing with her toes. "Rebecca, can you believe it? We're in Amsterdam at last!"

A maid knocked on the door. She was carrying a large kettle of warm water. She poured the water into a basin on the washstand, placed clean towels and clothes on the bed, and left the room. Johanna gave Rebecca a bath, and changed her diaper and dress. Then she put Rebecca on the rug so she could wash herself and change her dress.

Using the bed as support, Rebecca tried to pull herself up to a standing position. But once she was standing, she didn't know how to get down again. She fell hard on her bottom and began to wail.

Johanna rushed over to the baby, picked her up, and sat down on the chair. "Shh, Rebecca," she crooned. "We're safe now."

The memories of her journey rushed through Johanna's mind. She remembered the people who had helped her on the way. Tears of gratitude welled in her eyes.

Holding the baby, Johanna rummaged in her bag for her comb. Instead, she touched the lace kerchief Mama had given her. She inhaled its faint fragrance and tucked it into her skirt.

There was a knock on the door. "Fraulein Eisen?" said Mrs. de Groot.

Johanna opened the door. "Yes?"

"Everyone is waiting. Please come down at once."

Before leaving the room, Johanna paused. Holding Rebecca tightly, she whispered, "Dear baby, you will grow up to be strong in this new land. And God willing, I will soon bring Mama here. We will make a new life for ourselves. We shall be free."

Johanna straightened her back and breathed deeply. She walked down the stairs to welcome the Sabbath day of rest and peace.

Acknowledgements

Thank you to writers and friends who gave suggestions, large and small, to help this book move from a small idea to the finished book: Rona Arato, Meryl Arbing, Rochelle Carrady, Peter Carver, Sharon MacKay, Mark Mazer, Judy Nisenholt, Michael Posluns, Linda Pruessen, Tom Sankey, Judy Saul, Liliane Schacter, Kathy Stinson, Sydell Waxman, Lynn Westerhout, and Frieda Wishinsky.

And thank you to experts who provided insights into the life and times of Germany and the Netherlands in the 1700s: Corey Keeble, Curator of European decorative arts, arms and armour, and sculpture, World Cultures, Royal Ontario Museum, Toronto; Wiebke Müller, Librarian, Museum für Hamburgische Geschichte, Hamburg; Doctor Yuval Shaked, The Feher Jewish Music Center, Beth Hatefutsoth, The Nahum Goldmann Museum of the Jewish Diaspora, Tel Aviv; Michael Simonson, Archivist, Leo Baeck Institute, New York; Doctor Barry D. Walfish, Judaica specialist, Thomas Fisher Rare Book Library, University of Toronto Library, Toronto.

Of course, final thanks go to the hardworking, professional staff at Dundurn Press who showed kindness and expertise throughout the process: Michael Carroll, Nicole Chaplin, and Courtney Horner.

More Great Teen Fiction

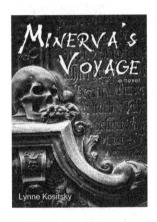

Minerva's Voyage
by Lynne Kositsky
978-1554884391
$12.99

Dragged off the streets of seventeenth-century England and on board a ship bound for Virginia by the murderous William Thatcher, Noah Vaile befriends a young cabin boy, Peter Fence. After being shipwrecked on the mysterious Isle of Devils, the two set off on an adventure filled with mystery, danger, villainy, and a treasure rarer and finer than gold.

Little Jane Silver
by Adira Rotstein
978-1554888788
$12.99

Little Jane Silver is the granddaughter of the notorious pirate Long John Silver. Growing up on her parents' ship, she vows to become a real pirate. As her ship is pursued by a mysterious pirate hunter, Little Jane tries to alert the crew to a devious saboteur on the ship, but by the time someone pays attention, it's too late.

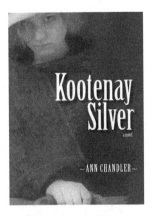

Kootenay Silver
by Ann Chandler
978-1554887552
$12.99

In 1910, twelve-year-old Addy McLeod waits in a cabin for her brother, Cask, to send for her. She must fight off the advances of her alcoholic stepfather, but then tragedy strikes. She flees and disguises herself as a boy as she journeys to find Cask, and herself, in the British Columbia silver town of Kaslo on Kootenay Lake.

DUNDURN
www.dundurn.com

What did you think of this book?
Visit www.dundurn.com for
reviews, videos, updates, and more!

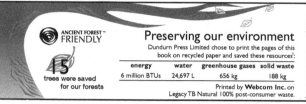